LET'S BAKE A DEAL

Twin Berry Bakery 2

WENDY MEADOWS

© 2020, Wendy Meadows

All rights reserved. No part of this publication may be reproduced, distributed or transmitted in any form or by any means, without prior written permission.

This is a work of fiction. Names, characters, places, and incidents are a product of the author's imagination. Locales and public names are sometimes used for atmospheric purposes. Any resemblance to actual people, living or dead, or to businesses, companies, events, institutions, or locales is completely coincidental.

Majestic Owl Publishing LLC
P.O. Box 997
Newport, NH 03773

1

Rita parked the SUV under a tall maple tree resplendent with red and yellow and orange leaves at the far end of a wide open field lined with rows and rows of parked vehicles leading up to the colorful tents and the fairway of the Pumpkin Festival. "My goodness, the festival is really packed," she said in amazement and quickly checked her makeup and hair in the rearview mirror.

"You look fine, stop fussing," said her twin sister Rhonda with a gentle roll of her eyes.

"I usually don't wear makeup but I thought a dash of blush and some light lipstick would look nice with my new dress."

Rhonda looked at her twin sister and grinned. She couldn't resist teasing her usually staid sister. "Well, that dress you're wearing would look nicer if it wasn't so...oh...loud."

Rita gasped. "My dress...what's wrong with my dress?" she asked in a worried voice, smoothing down the understated damask dress with velvet ribbon trim patterned in autumn colors and motifs. "I thought a nice dress with leaves and pumpkins would look...nice."

Rhonda suppressed a giggle. She loved teasing her sister. "Oh, I suppose it's...nice," she said and checked her own hair. Excited to get to the fair that day, Rhonda had tied her hair into a sensible ponytail while Rita had spent a painstaking hour in front of the mirror, opting for loose waves framing her face in a relaxed tumble.

"And I suppose you think that...that monstrosity you're wearing is...nice," Rita asked, feeling her cheeks flush red. "You look like a...a..."

"Khaki pumpkin?" Rhonda laughed. She buttoned up her soft orange cardigan over her comfortable tan knit dress that swirled below her knees, checking the wind that rustled the leaves outside. "Go ahead, you were saying…?"

"Oh," Rita fussed, "nothing bothers you."

Rhonda patted Rita's hand. "Your dress is lovely," she promised and tipped a sweet wink. "You know I'm only teasing you."

Rita sighed. "I should have known...but with you it's difficult to tell at times," she said and nudged Rhonda gently with her elbow. "My dress really is nice?" She looked down again at the swirling colors as excited as a young girl.

"Really nice," Rhonda confirmed. She shouldered her white purse and they climbed out of the vehicle and looked around. "I can't believe we're in the middle of the Pumpkin Festival already," she said. "I thought we'd make it over here during the first week, but no…luckily Erma was able to mind the bakery for us."

"Our bakery which is a smashing success," Rita supplied with a proud nod of her head.

"We have the entire day to ourselves. A day to stroll around the fairgrounds, sip apple cider, buy pumpkins, enjoy all the arts and crafts, eat pumpkin pie, smell the fresh autumn air, watch the leaves fall, get lost in the corn maze, and have a blast." Rhonda was halfway to the entrance gate before she realized her sister was lagging behind.

Rita was looking inside her light green purse with a slightly guilty look. "I brought three hundred dollars," she confessed. "I know we're supposed to be watching our pennies, but our bakery is bringing in such a surprising profit…I wanted to spoil myself."

"This coming from Ms. Rationality," Rhonda pointed out and tipped Rita another wink.

"I know, I know," Rita sighed. "I've been watching every penny we've been spending like a hawk. And now look at me. I'm throwing this much money into the wind?" Rita zipped her purse carefully and double-checked it before she hurried forward to walk next to her sister. "Our bakery's success has been such a Godsend…it's all the recipes Erma gave us! Every one has turned out amazing. I guess we were right after all to stick with the vintage nineteen-thirties look…everyone in town says it feels just like it used to back when Erma's family ran the bakery, and they love that our baked goods taste like what she used to bake, too!

"That woman has the touch," Rhonda said in a happy voice.

"She has certainly turned our bakery into something very special," Rita agreed as leaves danced in a crisp morning wind. Across the field she could smell apple cider, fresh hay bales, and pumpkin pie mixed with hot funnel cakes, boiled peanuts, and corn on the cob. She could see rows and rows of arts and crafts booths and the murmurs of the happy crowds wandering from place to place. A tractor rumbled along pulling a hayride along the far edge of the field where the corn maze was situated. Everything simply sang of fall and fun. A huge smile spread across Rita's face as her steps quickened toward the entrance gate of the festival.

"Boy, what's gotten into you," her sister Rhonda commented with amusement.

"I promised myself I would stop penny pinching when the right time came," Rita explained, "and that time is now! I've been so uptight over our finances, what with moving here to a new town and starting a new business, to the point that I began dreading our new life instead of embracing it alongside you."

"I know," Rhonda replied and let out a heavy breath. "I watch you do the books."

Rita winced a little. "I've been pretty tense."

"Just a tad," Rhonda agreed and then let a warm smile slip back across her face. "Rita, you saw our first bank deposit. We're fine. As a matter of fact, we're more than fine." Rhonda patted her own wallet in her purse. "Why shouldn't we get to spend a couple hundred at the fair?" she asked. "As much as your rational tendencies annoy me, I do respect them. I respect that you're very cautious over our business spending and that you want to keep us in the green."

"You mean the black?" Rita said, puzzled. "In accounting, you want to be in the black…"

Her sister laughed and rolled her eyes good-naturedly. "Whatever. This is exactly why I feel comfortable spending money today, because I know we're fine and are going to continue being fine. Even when you stop penny-pinching, your eyes will still be on the bottom line. And we're both very smart gals who understand when it's okay to spend and when it's time to be careful."

Rita looked at her sister and felt a grateful love swell in her heart. Sure, Rhonda could be a clown at times and loved to make jokes. But Rhonda was also a woman who knew how to use her brain and be smart. If she was willing to trust Rita, that meant that the sisters truly had no worries about money. "Let's go have a wonderful day."

"You bet," Rhonda giggled and hurried along the grass in

the morning air. "Beat you to the gate!" The two sisters laughed as they hurried along.

Oh, will you smell that!" Rhonda exclaimed when they entered the fairgrounds. "Crisp air...pumpkins...fresh burning wood..." Rhonda swung her gaze around in every direction and absorbed the soft beauty of the morning. "Oh, I could just melt."

"I know," Rita smiled as the winds began playing in her strawberry blonde hair. She tried to forget her nervousness about her dress and the makeup she was unaccustomed to wearing—although many people who saw them thought the twin sisters were quite beautiful. "Fresh chimney smoke from nearby homes...oh, this is so wonderful."

Rhonda grabbed Rita's hand. "Let's hurry before all the good stuff is taken," she begged and pointed down at her feet. "I wore my running shoes because I plan to do a whole lot of walking."

"I wore my running shoes, too," Rita giggled and checked her watch. "Okay, it's almost ten. The festival has been running since nine and doesn't close until nine tonight. That leaves us eleven hours. I think that's enough time to walk our legs off."

"Then what are we waiting for," Rhonda exclaimed and began dragging Rita down a long row of booths. "Oh, that food smells so good."

"I'll buy you a hot apple cider," Rita promised.

"And a funnel cake?" Rhonda laughed. "Today I'm kicking my healthy diet to the wind." Rhonda dragged Rita past a massive wooden pumpkin painted with the festival sign near the ticket booth. Two older women manned a table by the entrance booth. Rhonda read out loud the sign attached to the table: "Pumpkin Raffle…one dollar a ticket...the grand prize is the Blue Ribbon Pumpkin."

"Oh, we have to enter," Rita pleaded with Rhonda.

"You bet your hot funnel cake we have to enter," Rhonda agreed and quickly yanked two singles from her purse. "Two raffle tickets, please."

Bertha Mills smiled, took Rhonda's money, placed it in an old-fashioned cash register, and said, "Two tickets it is."

Allison Light, a sweet, elderly black woman, smiled at Bertha, peeled two orange tickets off a thick roll, and handed them to Rita. "Here you go, dears, good luck."

Rita quickly handed Rhonda a ticket and beamed at Bertha and Allison. It was clear the two old women were lifelong friends who had been through thick and thin together. "Thank you so much," she said.

Allison smiled. "You two girls own Erma's bakery now, right?"

"Yes, ma'am, we sure do," Rhonda replied in an exuberant voice. "Twin Berry Bakery is up and running."

"Erma is watching the bakery for us today," Rita explained as a line of people began forming behind them. "We needed a day off to enjoy the festival...anyway, thank you again. We'll be going now. Bye."

"Bye, dear," Allison smiled and waved at Rita and Rhonda as they walked under the large wooden pumpkin and entered the fairgrounds.

"My, so many people and it's not even lunch," Rhonda gasped as her eyes soaked in rows and rows of arts and crafts tables, food stands, game booths and even a few rides set up for children to enjoy. A pony walked in a hay-strewn paddock for children to ride, along with a camel for the more adventurous, and a small petting zoo with goats and sheep had been set up to one side. "The festival sure is in full swing."

Rita locked her eyes on a game booth. The booth held four large pumpkins with tall stems. Small children were trying to toss orange, red, and brown plastic rings around the stems. An old man who appeared to be in his late seventies sat inside the booth smiling at the children, smoking a worn cherrywood pipe and watching them play; no cheap carnival gags and tricks here, just simple, innocent, free, games where the winner could win a ticket for a cup of apple cider, or a funnel cake, or a hayride, or other sweet gifts that touched the heart. "I love Clovedale Falls," she told Rhonda in a dear voice. "I'm falling in love with this town more and more each day."

"I know what you mean," Rhonda agreed and pointed to a promising stand. An older woman was holding out a thick, paper plate with hot funnel cake dipped in peppermint sprinkles to a young girl. The young girl looked up at her mom and dad. The dad smiled and nodded his head. The girl happily took hold of it, thanked the old woman, and took a bite. Her face lit up with joy.

"No video games...no technology...no politics...just people enjoying community fun and nature. The true gifts that the good Lord offers us...if we're willing to accept them, that is."

Rita hooked her arm through Rhonda's and pointed to a hot apple cider stand. "Let's go get us some, and then visit each and every arts and crafts booth."

"I'm with you."

Rita walked Rhonda up to the drink stand, with a front counter framed in wood carved and painted in the shape of large apple. They smiled at a short, chubby woman dressed in a red apple costume, with an apple-blossom patterned apron. The woman hurried over to Rita and Rhonda. "Lucy, you look terrific," Rita laughed.

Lucy Whitson gave a polite curtsey. "In the off season I'm Lucy Whitson, cashier," she said in a dramatic voice. "During the Pumpkin Festival, I'm Lucy Whitson, Apple Woman Extraordinaire!"

Rhonda began clapping her hands. "Bravo," she laughed.

Lucy laughed too, tucking her black curls away from her eyes, and pointed at the long wooden table behind her. "We have hot or cold apple cider, peach cider, and pear cider, along with apple and peach slushies. What will you ladies have?"

Rita and Rhonda studied the row of cups and the sign and then focused on two slushy machines. One was marked Apple, churning a cold, icy mixture the color of apple cider, and the other was labeled Peach, and a delectable color of peachy pink. "I've never had fruit slushy before," Rita confessed.

"Me neither," Rhonda added. She looked at her sister. "Shall we be daring and come back for a hot apple cider later?"

Rita bit down on her lower lip, thought for a few seconds, and then nodded. "Let's try something new. Two apple cider slushies, please."

Lucy smiled. "I thought you two might be adventuresome," she said and hurried to dispense them, "My husband is supposed to be helping me," she called out, picking up two tall red cups, "but he wandered off to talk to Fred Johnson again. Sometimes being married to that man is impossible. And just try running a grocery store with him. Don't get me started."

Rita and Rhonda grinned at each other. Not a day went by that Lucy didn't complain about her husband. Lucy and her husband were very much in love, however. "If we spot Fred we'll send him back your way," they promised.

"Please do," Lucy begged as she finished filling one of the red cups.

Rita began to respond but stopped when she saw Billy Northfield standing outside of a large orange tent with his hands shoved down into the pockets of his overalls, looking bored but interested at the same time. "There's Billy," she told Rhonda and pointed in his direction. He was talking to a man who, as far as Rita and Rhonda could tell, might have been a brother. However, Billy didn't have a brother.

Rhonda spotted Billy and smiled. There was something very special about him that she held dear in her heart. "Let's go over and say hello to him."

"Okay," Rita agreed. "Lucy, how much do we owe you?"

"Two dollars apiece," Lucy said and handed Rita and Rhonda their slushies. Rita quickly dug into her purse and paid Lucy. "We'll see you later, okay? Save some hot cider for us!"

"Okay," Lucy smiled and turned to greet the next family approaching the booth.

They walked away from the booth, paused, and looked down at their drinks. Neither had even touched their straw. "Well...we did pay for these," she said.

"We sure did," Rhonda agreed and bit down on her lip. "Ready?" Rita nodded her head. "Okay...one...two...three..." Rhonda quickly took a sip of slushy and then beamed all over. "Hey, this is delicious."

"It sure is," Rita agreed and took another sip. "My goodness...delicious."

Rhonda took a bigger sip. "That Lucy, she's been holding out on us," she said in a silly spy voice. "We will have to tickle her with a feather until she reveals her secrets."

Rita laughed. "Come on, silly. Let's go say hello to Billy and--" Rita paused.

"What?" Rhonda asked.

"Look," Rita whispered and nodded her head toward the orange tent.

Rhonda turned her eyes toward the tent. At first, Billy was the only familiar face she saw, and then Sheriff Bluestone's face appeared. "Oh, it's Brad."

"No way," Rita objected. "Brad might ask us to...go direct traffic or something. Come on." Rita grabbed Rhonda's hand and began pulling her away into the crowd. As she did, Brad looked up with interest at the pair. "Oh no, he's spotted us."

Brad threw his hand into the air to wave at the ladies and began making his way over to them. "We can't be rude, Rita," Rhonda whispered. "Brad probably just wants to say hello."

Rita watched Brad hurry through the crowd toward them. "Not with that expression," she whispered back.

Rhonda locked her eyes on Brad's face. She had to admit the man was wearing a very serious expression that was out of character for such a joyous festival. "We'll just...say hello," she hesitantly said.

"I doubt it," Rita whispered again, dreading the news Brad might bring.

"Ladies," Brad said approaching both sisters, "Erma told me I would be able to find you here."

"Enjoying a lovely morning at the festival. As civilians," Rita quickly pointed out.

"Yes, peaceful civilians," Rhonda added as she read Brad's eyes. Something was wrong and despite the sunshine in the sky, the man was about to bring in the rain.

"Ladies," Brad said and eased his eyes around, "I'm going to have to cancel your morning. I need you to step into your peacekeeping roles as investigators again. There's been a..." Brad looked around once more and lowered his voice. "There's been a murder."

Rita nearly dropped her slushy. Rhonda let out a deep moan. "Oh no," they both whined at the same time and looked down at the ground. So much for a fun-filled morning—their morning suddenly felt clouded with tragedy and it was about to turn very, very strange.

Brad drove Rita and Rhonda out to the Clovedale Falls Retirement Home, located on a hundred and five beautiful acres of clean, crisp mountain land outside the main town. As he drove down a winding road hugging the banks of a softly flowing river, Brad explained the situation. "Rusty Lowly is eighty years old," he began while they sat in the back seat of his car sipping their slushies. "Rusty suffers from memory loss. There are times, I've been told, when he can tell you the score of the sandlot baseball game he played on a certain afternoon when he was five years old, and then there are times when he can't even remember his own name."

"And you think this old man is a murderer?" Rita asked Brad in a skeptical voice.

"Rusty was found standing over the body of a very wealthy woman named Lynn Hogan," Brad replied in a sorrowful voice. "Lynn was stabbed to death and Rusty was holding the murder weapon." Brad eased off the gas pedal to allow them more time to talk. "Nurse Patricia Taylor found Rusty standing in Lynn Hogan's room, right over the poor woman's body, holding the knife."

Rhonda glanced out of the back seat window and spotted the river glittering between the colorful autumn trees. She sighed. "Brad, this sounds like a terrible tragedy. But why do you need us? This seems like a pretty open and shut case. Why drag us into it? You seem perfectly capable of dealing with a case like this. Besides, my sister and I were enjoying a beautiful morning…"

Brad eased off the gas pedal even more, spotted a gravel area on the side of the road with two picnic tables, and eased to a stop next to them. "Now we've made him mad," Rita whispered to Rhonda.

"No, you haven't made me mad," Brad explained. He opened the driver's side door, got out, walked over to a picnic table, retrieved his pipe, and looked at the river. Rita and Rhonda shrugged their shoulders and made their way out of the car and over to Brad. "Ladies," Brad said and began fishing in his pocket for a box of matches, "Rusty Lowly is a retired cop. He worked the streets for forty years…retiring probably about the same time you ladies decided to become cops." Brad found the matches and lit his pipe, puffing into the quiet air. "I trained with Rusty for many years, but I'm the only one left in these parts who knows him from back then. I know he isn't a killer. Proving that to a jury…that's a different problem."

Rita and Rhonda listened to Brad with intent ears and then looked at each other. "That's where we come in," they said.

Brad nodded his head. "My guys aren't practiced enough to conduct a thorough homicide investigation," he said puffing on his pipe. The smell of cherry tobacco danced around, touched Rita and Rhonda's noses, and then wandered off down to the river. "My guys would probably bungle half the evidence. If I report this murder to the suits, they'll investigate it for me just fine, but they'll also force me to arrest Rusty. I ain't ready to do that…not now, not ever. Even if it means laying down my badge…then so be it."

Rita walked over to a wooden trash can and tossed her cup inside. Then she turned her full attention to Brad. "How can you be so sure Mr. Lowly didn't kill Lynn Hogan?"

Brad perched his foot up on the bench of the picnic table and locked his eyes on the glittering river. "Rusty Lowly isn't a killer," he replied in a gruff voice. "I know the man."

Rhonda discarded her cup too and then sat down at the picnic table. "You believe Mr. Lowly was framed, or confused, don't you?" she asked Brad.

"You better believe it. He might be losing his memory, but a senile person doesn't just turn into a cold-blooded murderer." His voice wobbled ever so slightly and he cleared his throat a little.

Rita sat down next to her sister. "Okay, Brad," she said in an honest voice, "cops stick together. We're on your side...even though being on your side has destroyed our morning."

"Being a good cop sure hurts," Rhonda agreed. She looked at Brad and forced her mind to change gears. The Pumpkin Festival would have to wait. A murder had taken place and a friend needed help. "Brad, who is this Lynn Hogan, anyway? How did she get so wealthy?"

"She is—was—a very wealthy widow," Brad told Rhonda as he puffed on his pipe. "Lynn Hogan is the heiress of an estate worth over four million dollars. Maybe more once her assets are sold."

"That's a lot," Rhonda admitted, "but we all know that's small change compared to the big-time money floating around out there."

Rita scratched the tip of her nose and then leaned forward. "What Rhonda is trying to say is that it doesn't seem that this was a crime hit. This could point more toward family or close friends."

"Yeah, I thought of that," Brad agreed. "That's why I'm running down Lynn Hogan's family as we speak."

"Good," Rita agreed.

"Does Mr. Lowly have any family?" Rhonda asked, feeling a tender breeze touch her face. Oh, the morning was so beautiful. It was such a waste to spend it on murder.

Brad shook his head no. "Rusty is a widower, he and his late wife never had kids. He became a real loner after he retired."

Rhonda looked at Rita. Rita nodded. "Brad, how much does it cost for a person to live at the Clovedale Falls Retirement Home?" she asked.

Brad lowered his pipe and looked at Rita with worried eyes. "More than a retired cop earns," he said in a sickened tone of voice. "Chump change for a woman like Lynn Hogan, but a tight squeeze for a man like Rusty."

Rhonda made a few quick mental notes and moved on. "What about the staff?" she asked. "Are any of the staff special friends with Rusty? Does anyone have a grudge against him? Who is his doctor?"

"All questions that will have to be answered," Rita told Brad. "We also need to know what time the murder took place, the whereabouts of each staff and community member, the works."

"I got it," Brad assured his friends. "I worked homicide, ladies, remember? You're not talking to a greenhorn."

"We know that Brad," Rita commented, "but we also know this case is hitting you on a personal level and sometimes emotions can cloud protocol. We've seen it happen before...even to us."

Brad puffed on his pipe. "Yeah, I've seen it happen before, too," he said and tossed a thumb toward his car. "We better get a move on."

"Sure," Rhonda agreed and they walked back to the car and climbed into the back seat. "What do you think?" she asked Rita, watching Brad empty out his pipe and then begin making his way around the front of the car.

"I'm not entirely sure yet," Rita confessed. "What I do know is that Brad is going to keep the suits out of this case as long as possible. Time surely isn't on our side, especially after Lynn Hogan's family is contacted. Who knows what kind of people they will be and what demands they will put on Brad and Clovedale Falls."

"Let's hope that this case will be an easy solve," Rhonda replied in a hopeful voice.

"Let's hope," Rita agreed as Brad jumped into the driver's seat and started moving down the highway. Ten minutes later he turned off of Peppermint Highway and took a left onto Candy Stripe Lane and began driving up what appeared to a mountain. "My, I didn't know the retirement home was so far out," Rita said as her eyes soaked in the sight of one gorgeous autumn tree after the next.

"There is a landing pad for a helicopter in case of emergencies," Brad explained crawling around a sharp bend. "The hospital in town doesn't have the equipment to deal with the bad stuff anyway. A medical chopper can get in and out and fly someone to a life-saving hospital a lot faster than we can transport them by ambulance."

"Makes sense, I guess," Rita replied.

"Folks choose peace and quiet," Brad explained. "I wouldn't want to live out the rest of my days next to a hospital out of fear that something might happen to me. When I can't live at home anymore I want my wife to stick me up here. In the peace and quiet of the woods."

Rhonda understood Brad's words. Even though she never thought about growing old enough to the point where she would never be able to take care of herself, she surely understood the need to have a place of serenity to live out the rest of her years, if that point in her life ever arrived. "It is very beautiful up here," she admitted. "I would want to spend the rest of my days somewhere where life is this beautiful, too."

Brad nodded. "The Clovedale Falls Retirement Home is quite some place," he explained. "The home sits on open land filled with streams, a river, a small park, flower beds, manicured lawns, walking paths, a tennis court...we're talking about some money." Brad eased around another sharp bend. "I've been around for a while, so I can give you all the history if you like. It was originally a private home, built in 1901 by a man named Michael Stonewell. Stonewell was a business man looking to retire from the world. He purchased the land and built a mansion...which was turned into the retirement home...and lived out the rest of his years in peace with his wife at his side. In 1928, Stonewell died and in 1930, his wife died. The Stonewells didn't have a will, strange as it sounds, and the courts were not able to locate any living descendants, so the property went to the city of Clovedale Falls. He always wanted to turn it into a home for the care of the elderly, he just never got around to writing his will I guess."

"That was a nice gesture," Rhonda commented.

"You could say that. I think his estate was barely enough to keep his wife fed and housed for her remaining years, and after that...I think the land and the building required so much upkeep...fixing it up would have cost more than it was worth. You have to remember very few people had money to waste on buying property, never mind fixing roofs and mulching rose gardens, not back in the Depression years," Brad said with a shrug.

Brad hit a straight lane and pressed down on the gas pedal just enough to bring the car up to a reasonable speed, making up their lost time. "Anyway, in the thirties and forties, the mansion was turned into a home for soldiers needing rehabilitation – World War I vets who required long-term care, things like that. During World War II, the mansion was put into use again as a retreat for soldiers sent home from the war with injuries, and after the war as well. Rehab, nursing, occupational help, whatever they needed. The city didn't keep the property up much, but there was such a great need for facilities at the time, it didn't matter if the roofs leaked a little or the fuse boxes went on the fritz every time the wind blew from the south. It wasn't until after the Korean War that the rehab folks left for good. The place was in very poor condition and the city was preparing to condemn the mansion and auction off the land, but a woman named Katherine Stein stepped in, bought the mansion and the land, turned it into what it is today, and left the place to the care of her daughter, Kathleen Stein—who goes by Kathy—she lives in Atlanta with her husband and children."

"Impressive," Rita told Brad. "You've done your research."

"Years ago I studied this place," he admitted. "My uncle was very sick and close to death and I was considering bringing him here. The cost was too high and I ended up sending him to a different place." Brad spotted the gray metal entrance gate up ahead and began to slow down. He continued, "but I became curious about the history of the retirement home and did some digging."

"Have you contacted Kathy Stein?" Rhonda asked Brad, watching him ease up to the security camera and coded entry pad at the gate.

"Not yet," Brad replied. "I don't want any outside interference until I get some answers."

"Good idea," Rhonda told Brad.

Brad nodded his head, stuck his hand out of the window, punched in a few numbers into the security pad, and waited for the gate to open. "This should be very interesting," Rita told Rhonda, watching the gate begin to ease open.

"You bet," Rhonda agreed.

"Here we go," Brad said and drove his car onto a smooth, one-lane road that began twisting and turning up one final large hill. The trees hugging the road suddenly gave way to clear, gorgeously landscaped grounds that took Rita and Rhonda's breath away. Rita spotted the sparkling river down the hill to her right. Beautiful, breathtaking flower gardens ran beside the river, with garden benches and a gazebo tucked next to walking paths that made her heart melt. Many were paved in order to accommodate wheelchairs, she noted. "Beautiful, isn't it?" Brad asked.

"I didn't know such a place existed," Rita replied, stunned by the beauty.

"My goodness," Rhonda whispered, staring at the green manicured lawns that sloped smoothly down to the river. It was like entering a completely different world.

Brad continued up the narrow road, twisting and turning, and then stopped atop the hill. "Let's get out," he said. "Wait till you see this," he grinned.

"Okay." They hurried out of the backseat and met Brad at the hood of the car. Brad raised his hand and pointed. "Oh my," they gasped, spotting an enormous mansion with little turret towers and porches everywhere. It was as big as a castle—a castle fit for a king. The sight of the mansion was enough to make a person wonder if they had somehow traveled back in time. "Are you sure Mr. Stonewell didn't build a castle?"

Brad stared at the mansion. "Ladies," he said in a very serious voice, "somewhere in that place lurks a killer...a real killer. And as you both can see, we're out in the world, all alone. You can't walk outside and call for help up here because help ain't coming this far out and this far up. We can't be the boy who cried wolf up here and whistle for an airlift ambulance at the first sign of trouble, understand?" Brad kept his eyes on the mansion. "My good friend Rusty Lowly is up there and he needs our help. Now, I know you're both professionals, but this case is going to take everything we have. Right now you need to put away the thought of your bakery, the festival, the town, everything, and focus on helping my good friend."

Rita and Rhonda studied the mansion with amazed eyes. "Brad," Rita said solemnly, "you have our attention."

"And we'll focus on this case. With expert concentration," Rhonda added. "But when this case is over we're selling our cabin and moving here. My goodness...so beautiful."

Brad took his eyes away from the mansion and looked at them, shaking his head with a roll of his eyes. "We better get up there, ladies."

Rita pulled her eyes away and gazed around the tenderly kept land surrounding the building. She didn't spot a single person. "I can imagine myself living up here alone, walking this land," she said. "Far away from the world...no people...no crime...no murders...only peace."

"Me too," Rhonda agreed. "Planting flowers, taking walks, reading books...so peaceful." Rhonda shook her head. "But even way up here, murder has a way of showing its ugly, stinking, miserable face."

"I know," Rita replied in a sickened voice. "Come on, Rhonda. We have work to do."

Brad nodded and led them walking up to the front doors of this massive estate holding an old man who couldn't remember if he killed Lynn Hogan or not. All he could remember was that it was getting near lunch and he was hungry.

2

Nurse Mae Taylor—known to her friends and patients only as Nurse Mae—opened the ornately carved front door that looked strong enough to keep a foreign army at bay. The carvings, depicting the ancestral family crest of the original owners, spoke of powerful wealth. "Sheriff, I thought you would never get back," Mae complained, ushering them in quickly.

"I know, I know," Brad said, walking into the large foyer with wood paneled walls painted in alternating red and white stripes like peppermint canes. The sight of the peppermint cane walls made Rita and Rhonda feel like they had entered an enchanted wonderland. Both women studied the foyer with amazed eyes. "We got held up for a few minutes."

Rita glanced down at a solid white marble floor that had an inlaid image of a single red peppermint exactly in the middle. The whole place was polished to a softly glowing shine. "Clovedale Falls Retirement Home sure does take its name seriously," she whispered to Rhonda.

Rhonda nodded. "I know, but it's so...cozy. This foyer is massive but I feel like I've walked into somebody's warm and welcoming home."

Nurse Mae looked at Rita and Rhonda with cautious eyes. She had heard about the twin retired policewomen who had recently moved to Clovedale Falls, but had yet to meet them. Of course, at the age of sixty-eight and with her nursing shifts keeping her busy, she didn't get around much and rarely left her place of work. She lived here, in fact, on the third floor in a private room paid through paycheck deductions. Mae didn't mind having money taken out of her paycheck—the mansion was her home and she intended to live there as a nurse and then retiring when she could no longer take care of her friends. She hoped these newcomers would understand the kind of care and dedication that went into this beloved place.

"My name is Patricia Taylor. You can call me Mae. I'm the head nurse," She explained in a stern voice. She didn't want to sound cold, but a woman in her care had been murdered and murder was serious business. Deep down, Mae was a soft teddy bear.

Rita examined Nurse Mae. The woman was tall and thin, with a lovely face and bright eyes that reminded her of the actress Vivian Vance. Her long, smooth gray hair was tucked neatly but not severely into a bun. She wore the red and white striped uniform scrub dress that all the staff wore, and the colors complimented Mae's lovely face.

Rita reached out to shake the nurse's hand. "My name is Rita Knight. This is my sister Rhonda Knight."

Rhonda offered Mae a friendly smile and saw the older woman's eyes darting back and forth between their two faces, trying to tell them apart. "Rita wears her hair down and I usually wear my hair in a ponytail," she explained. "If you're wondering how you can tell us apart."

Brad scratched the back of his neck. He still had a hard time telling Rita and Rhonda apart and referred to them as 'Ladies' when they were together instead of trying to single them out by name. "Mae, these are two ladies that I trust. I wouldn't have brought them here if I didn't."

Mae looked at Rhonda and then back at Rita. The twin sisters were surely beautiful, she thought, and their eyes did hold a sweet sense of honesty that was rare to see in the younger generation. "You have to understand my position," she explained, easing her voice down a notch. "A woman is dead, and a very dear friend...was found in the dead woman's room." Mae threw a desperate look at Brad. "I still won't believe Rusty killed Lynn," she exclaimed in an upset voice. "Rusty wouldn't hurt a soul."

Brad looked around. "Doc Downing is still in surgery over in Hayfield," he explained. "He won't be back in town for another two hours."

Mae folded her arms together. "The body," she said and felt a cold shiver walk down her spine, "is still in the walk-in freezer. I doubt it's going anywhere."

Rhonda looked at Brad and studied his face with intent

eyes. "You haven't notified anyone of this murder, have you? Not even your own guys."

"Nope," Brad answered in an honest and clear voice. "I have some locals helping out my guys with the traffic and parking for the festival and I ain't taking the chance of letting one of my guys slip up and tell a local that there's been a murder. If that happens, word of the murder will spread like wildfire and that could hurt business and we'd have everybody up here gawking in no time. No, it's better to keep this as quiet as possible."

"In other words, people have big mouths around here," Mae said, feeling creepy all over.

"Yep," Brad nodded his head. "Doc Downing is the only man I know who can keep a secret in this town."

Rita and Rhonda glanced at each other. It was strange to be forced to work within someone else's jurisdiction and methods, like a vault trapping them in the dark. "Brad, we're breaking every rule in the book here," Rita pointed out in a worried voice. "There are still state and federal rules we have to adhere to when a murder—"

"I know that," Brad interrupted, "and right now I could care less about rules created by a bunch of bureaucrats. My job is to protect a close friend and I intend to do that, with or without you."

Rhonda patted Rita's hand. "Brad, we're on your side," she reminded him in a steady voice. "My sister is worried that we could end up in hot water and to be honest, so am I.

But," Rhonda glanced around, "for now we'll play by your rulebook."

"Appreciate it," Brad nodded his head and peered up the magnificent yet empty staircase of ornately carved wood. The stairs were covered in a red and white runner, alternating each step to continue the peppermint theme of the entire place. "Okay, ladies, here's the layout of this place. There are four levels and a basement." Brad walked Rita and Rhonda to the staircase. "The first level is the public area...kitchen, dining room, library, reading room, multi-purpose room, arts and crafts room, music room...stuff like that. The second floor is the living area for the residents. The third floor is the staff floor...offices, supply rooms—"

"And my personal room," Mae pointed out. "I'm the only full-time staff member, as well as the only staff member allowed to live on-site."

Brad nodded. "The fourth level is the attic, mainly storage." Brad looked up the staircase. "The layout is a little unique," he continued. "Each level practically a maze...lots of different hallways opening to different rooms. Not your average kind of house where all the rooms open up to a central hallway. Only the basement and the attic are normal."

"It's all Michael Stonewell's touch," Mae explained. "The man who built this home was a very curious man. No one really knows why he designed his home like a maze." Mae looked to her left and gestured at a hallway. "It took me a while to learn my hallways," she confessed. "The residents still have a difficult time."

Rita and Rhonda glanced down the hallway, saw it dead-end at a suit of armor. The polished metal figure held a peppermint striped flag. The hallway branched off to the left and right. The carpet runner down the center of the hallway swirled with red and white paisley. "Each floor is different," Brad continued. "So don't go thinking you have the layout figured out once you get the hang of one of the floors."

"Got it," Rita assured Brad and nudged Rhonda with her elbow. "My sister loves mazes, isn't that right?"

Rhonda grinned. "As a matter of fact, I do," she confessed. "Although," she added, "I have yet to find my way out of a corn maze without getting lost first."

Mae glanced up the stairs. "I drew a diagram of the floors when I first began working here," she explained. "Over time...once I learned my way...I stopped using it. I suppose I can try and draw one for you by memory if you'd like? We never did get around to posting up signs on the walls. All the staff know their way around by now."

"Maybe that wouldn't be such a bad idea," Rita suggested and then pointed out: "It's very possible that the killer knows the layout of this mansion by heart. There's no sense in us walking around at a disadvantage."

"I agree," Rhonda added. She looked around, studied the peppermint designs, and then nodded her head. "Brad, I think the first thing we should do is talk to Rusty Lowly."

"I'll take you to Rusty's room," Mae spoke up. "He's a tad grumpy because his lunch is late. I have Beth and Noel in the kitchen making soup and sandwiches for everyone."

"Soup and sandwiches sounds good," Rhonda told Mae and rubbed her stomach, remembering the long-ago cider slushy. "I could eat."

Mae placed her hands together and hesitated. "Rhonda...right?"

"Yes?"

"We have ten residents at this home," Mae explained gently but firmly. "Each resident is on a special diet, which means that each meal has to be prepared differently. Beth is a certified medical chef and Noel is a certified nutritionist."

"I kinda guessed the folks here weren't ordering double cheese pizza every night," Rhonda joked and nudged Rita with her arm. "Old folks getting down on some pizza," she laughed.

Rita quickly widened her eyes at her sister. "Now isn't the time to be joking around," she whispered.

"Oh...sorry," Rhonda said and cleared her throat. "You were saying?" she asked.

"I was saying that if you want to something to eat, be prepared to eat foods that have very low sodium, no cholesterol, and...to be honest...very little taste." Mae let out a heavy sigh. "Our residents aren't very adventurous when it comes to flavors. Also, be prepared to tangle with two very cold women."

"Cold?" Rita asked.

"Beth and Noel might be certified in their fields of expertise," Mae explained, "but they're colder than ice floating in the arctic ocean. I don't why Kathy hired them. Our last chef, Ollie, was a wonderful man. Oh, he was so funny and always had a kind word to say. He served his meals with love." Mae's face turned sad. "Patty Olson was our nutritionist back then. Patty was a woman who made this world golden. It broke my heart to see her go."

"Maybe they eloped together," Rhonda said, laughing. "Sorry," she said again when her sister shot her a scowl.

"Why did Ollie and Patty leave?" Rita asked.

Mae shrugged her shoulders. "They never told me. A couple of months ago Mr. Rooney accepted a job in Maine and regretted that he couldn't give us a proper two weeks' notice. Ms. Olson resigned her position on the same day, said she had to move back west to help her sick mother."

"Mae, are Beth and Noel related, by chance?" Rita asked. Brad fished out his pipe and fiddled with the bowl of it, tapping it clean while he waited for Mae to answer.

"I don't know," Mae honestly answered. "Beth's last name is Frammer and Noel's last name is McGuire." Mae looked at Rita and Rhonda. "All I do know is that they're both from the Atlanta area."

Rhonda rubbed her chin. "How old are these two gals?" she asked, feeling a hint of Billy in her voice.

"Beth is...forty-one, I believe," Mae answered, searching her memory. "Noel is...let's see if I remember correctly...oh yes, she just had a birthday, so she must be forty-three."

"Are either of them married? Any children?" Rita asked.

Mae shrugged her shoulders. "I don't know. Kathy sent them to me on the very day Ollie and Patty quit. Kathy was the one who told me Ollie and Patty had called her to turn in their notice and..." Mae made a pained expression.

"What?" Rita gently pressed.

"Ollie and Patty are good people," Mae insisted. "They loved each person at this home. They would never just up and leave without a good reason." Mae looked over her shoulders and lowered her voice. "I'm going to confess...something that has been eating at my heart. I don't know if I can trust you, but if Brad brought you here...then maybe I can."

Rita and Rhonda studied Mae's troubled eyes and waited. There was no point in trying to assure Mae—trust had to be earned through time, not on the foundation of words. "Go ahead, Mae," Brad urged.

Mae looked over her shoulder again. "Beth and Noel give me the creeps," she whispered. "Those two women make my skin crawl." Mae moved closer to Rita and Rhonda, lowering her voice. "I've known Kathy Stein for years. I thought she was a good woman. Kathy would never in a million years hire two people like Beth and Noel. Her momma had a heart of gold and Kathy ain't too far behind in that department herself. That woman honestly cares about each person living here as much as the place itself. So why would she hire them? It doesn't make sense. Something doesn't add up about it." Mae looked into Rita and Rhonda's eyes. "It does cost a pretty penny to live here, I won't deny that. But there's something you don't know about the money that the folks pay to live here."

"What's that?" Rita asked.

Mae nodded at Brad. "You don't even know this, Brad, so listen to my words very carefully." Brad stepped closer to Mae. Mae glanced over her shoulder one last time. "Every penny that isn't spent on food, bills, maintenance, and so on, is sent straight to a charity to end hunger right here in the United States. The charity is located right in Atlanta." Mae studied the three faces staring at her. "Kathy doesn't make a penny off this place. The money she uses is really money spent to fulfill Miss Katherine's promise and nothing more."

"What promise?" Rhonda asked.

"Miss Katherine begged her daughter to keep this beautiful home and the land just the way her heart always wanted it to be," Mae explained. "A home for the elderly to live out their lives in peace and beauty. Miss Katherine loved this place...she even lived here, in the very room I live in now. Cancer took her home to the Lord when she was eighty...oh, she was a gift to all of us."

Rita looked at Rhonda. Rhonda did some quick math. "That would make Kathy Stein—"

"Forty-four," Mae explained. "Miss Katherine had Kathy late in life." Mae sighed. "Seems that might run in their family, though. There was a time when it seemed that Kathy herself wasn't going to be able to have children, but then all of sudden she became pregnant with two twin boys who were born bright, healthy, and beautiful, but a bit late in her life. That was...oh...seven years ago...so Kathy would have been almost the same age that her mother Katherine was when she had Kathy." Mae motioned up the staircase with her right hand. "Kathy was born in the very room I live in, in fact. She grew up in this house...she saw how much the people here and these walls meant to her mother. And that's why Kathy is keeping her promise."

Rita and Rhonda looked into Mae's eyes and saw the woman fighting back tears. Suddenly the Clovedale Falls Retirement Home became more than just a place for old people to live out their final days—the home's heartbeat whispered of a legacy and hidden secrets from the past. "I think we should talk to Rusty now," Rhonda said and gently patted Mae's hand.

Rusty Lowly eased up from a green armchair beside an oval lead-glass window. He held a confused expression consuming a wrinkled face that had been worn down by his many years. "Who are you?" he asked in a worried tone. "Are you from the bank?"

Rita and Rhonda both felt their heart break at the same time. They didn't see a killer. All they saw was a lonely, confused old man in the same brown pants and vest he had probably been wearing since the nineteen-sixties. "No, we're not from the bank," Rita said in a soft voice.

Rusty stared at Rita and then eased back down into his chair and straightened the old fashioned wide collar of his button-down shirt. The blue stripes of the shirt were as pale as the man's watery eyes as he looked up at them. "I paid my mortgage," he confessed. Rita in a confident yet wavering tone. "I paid every single payment on time. Ask your manager."

Rhonda glanced at Brad. Brad lowered his eyes down, overwhelmed with embarrassment and respect. The soft burgundy carpet of the man's room muffled the sound of Brad shuffling his feet for a moment as he cleared his throat. He looked up at the walls hung with mementos of Rusty's lifetime of police work; awards, commendations, framed newspaper clippings, a shadowbox with his old badge, even a blue and white uniform hat from his old patrol days. "Rusty, these two ladies are friends of mine," he finally said in a low voice.

"The bank don't send friends to your house," Rusty told Brad. "No sir, not when the bank wants your house." Rusty reached out his right hand and grabbed a polished, worn wooden cane leaning against the arm of his chair. "Get off my property," he said in a huff and began shaking the cane at Rita. "I paid my mortgage. You got no right, friends or no friends."

Rita felt her heart break all over again. She threw a glance at Rhonda and silently begged for help. Rhonda nodded and took over. "Mr. Lowly, I'm from the bank," she said in a steady voice. Brad raised his head and gave Rhonda a confused look.

"Ah, see?" Rusty said in a worried voice, "I knew the bank was going to send someone to take my home."

"I'm not here to take your home," Rhonda softly assured Rusty, seeing that the man was trapped in a painful memory that he couldn't escape. "I've come to tell you that the bank received your last mortgage payment and you're all paid up. Congratulations."

Rusty stared at Rhonda and then, to her relief, he slowly lowered his cane. "I sent in my mortgage payments," he insisted.

"Yes, all of them," Rhonda smiled even though within her heart she was fighting back tears. "You're all paid up, Mr. Lowly. No worries. Your house is yours forever and no one can take it away from you. Not now, not ever."

"Promisc?" Rusty asked.

"Cross my heart," Rhonda smiled again, staring kindly down into the man's wary blue eyes under his drooping eyelids. Knowing that her tears were about to fall, Rhonda quickly changed the subject. She pointed to a large bed in the middle of the room. The bed had a white and red curtain hung around it for privacy. "My, that's some bed," she said.

Rusty looked at the bed. "My Pauline...my wife...she liked peppermint," he explained, his demeanor turning nostalgic and sunny, completely forgetting about the bank. Inside his memories he saw a beautiful young woman of twenty-two sewing the bed curtain together in a cozy sewing room. "Pauline sewed that bed curtain for us one winter...it was snowing."

Rita walked over to the bed curtain and gently touched it with loving hands. "It's very beautiful."

"We lived in Minneapolis when we first got married," Rusty explained, cutting time away with a clear, sharp blade—yet, he couldn't remember what time it was. Wasn't it lunch? Wasn't he hungry? He couldn't remember. "I became a cop there...years later we moved to Chattanooga, Tennessee, to be close to Pauline's brother who had taken a job there. Pauline's folks were hard people and didn't care much for having Pauline around."

"Oh, I'm very sorry to hear that," Rhonda told Rusty.

Rusty put his cane down and made a sour face. "Pauline and her brother were better off in Chattanooga," he assured Rhonda. "We all missed Minneapolis at first, but by then I was already pushing forty and Pauline's folks were close to the grave. It was better to get some fresh air in a new place."

Brad slowly pulled out his pipe and lit it. "Rusty, maybe we better come back later, huh?" he asked. "Are you tired, old friend?"

Rusty looked at Brad. The man's face looked so familiar

yet he couldn't bring up a name. "You a friend of Chris's?" he asked. "Chris had lots of friends. He was a salesman, you know and—" Rusty let out a dry cackle. "That man could sell dirt to a groundhog. Boy howdy, could he. Why, one time, that rascal sold me some insurance that I didn't even need...tongue of gold, that one."

"Who's Chris?" Rita asked.

"Pauline's brother, of course," Rusty answered Rita, looking at her like she was crazy for asking such a question. "Man had a lovely wife but..." Rusty shook his head, "poor guy couldn't have kids, just like me and Pauline. Shame." Rusty looked at Brad again. "You friends with Chris?"

"No, I don't think so," Brad answered in an uncomfortable voice. He lowered his head and puffed on his pipe.

"Chris and Maggie adopted a boy all the way from Russia," Rusty said, returning his attention back to Rita. "When the boy grew up he went back to Russia...how is that for a thank you? Shame, shame."

Rhonda glanced at Rita. Rita was looking at Rusty with loving eyes, paying attention to his every word as if she were his dearest and closest friend. "That is a shame," Rita agreed with Rusty, holding her tongue about his strange, wandering stories. For now, she knew they had to let Rusty talk about anything and everything, in hopes of turning up a clue that would be helpful.

Rusty began to speak again but his words trailed off, his memories slipping away into a dark hole. He sat silent, staring into thin air, trying to remember what in the world he had been talking about. Then his eyes locked on Brad with sudden clarity. "Brad?" he asked in surprise.

Brad's head shot up. "Yeah, Rusty, I'm here." Grateful his old friend was coming around.

Rusty sniffed the air. "You smoking that pipe of yours again?"

"Yeah, hope you don't mind."

"You old flirt, you know my Pauline loves the smell of a pipe," Rusty smiled. He floated his eyes over to Rita and Rhonda. "Who are you two?" he asked.

"I'm Rita Knight," Rita smiled at Rusty.

"And I'm Rhonda Knight," Rhonda said and tossed a loving smile at Rusty. "My sister and I are with the police."

"You two are cops?" Rusty asked and then became excited. "Why, I was a cop for over forty years. I worked in Minneapolis and Chattanooga." Rusty slowly raised his body up from the chair, stumped his cane with him across the floor, and walked over to the police hat and uniform hanging on the wall. "This was my dress uniform," he announced in a proud voice. "By golly, they don't make uniforms like this anymore…or cops, for that matter."

"They sure don't, Rusty," Brad agreed.

Rusty nodded and moved onto a small wooden shadowbox hanging on the wall. "Know what's in this one?" he asked.

"No, we sure don't," Rhonda answered.

"A bullet," Rusty explained in a brave voice. "I was shot in the shoulder a few months before I retired," he continued and then let out a dry husk of a laugh. "Served my entire life as a cop and got shot just a few months before it was time for me to hang up my badge, how is that for irony?" Rusty tapped the wooden box with his cane. "I was shot by a drunk," he said and laughed again. "I guess that fella started celebrating my retirement too early, huh?"

"I guess so," Rita agreed.

"Being shot is no laughing matter," Rhonda pointed out.

"You're not lying. This was no small potatoes, either," Rusty told Rhonda as he stared at the little wooden box and the metal slug inside it. "The fella who shot me was one of them hard men who hurt lots of people. I went to serve a warrant on him and he answered the door with a gun. Good thing I was able to get to my own gun or I wouldn't be standing here—" Rusty paused. Another slow, dark cloud loomed in the distance. "I got my gun...and I shot the fella...it was me or him..." Rusty trudged with laborious steps back over to his chair, sat down, and looked at the heavy white drape pulls to one side of the oval window. "Yeah, it was me or him," he said and withdrew into silence. The cloud covered over his mind, dark and silent.

Rita nodded toward the hallway. Rhonda agreed and without saying a word to Rusty slipped out into the hallway with her sister and waited for Brad. "Rhonda, we can't let that old man take the fall for this murder," Rita said in an urgent voice. "He barely knows what year it is, and he can't remember a name five minutes after he learns it."

"Now I understand why Brad is breaking all the rules," Rhonda told Rita and let out a heavy breath. "I don't feel so bad if we're going to have to break a few rules on this one, either."

"Well," Rita pointed out, peering down the hallway that branched confusingly in three different directions not far from where they stood, "we're not officially cops anymore, Rhonda. The rules don't apply to us, technically."

"But the law does," Rhonda replied and then rolled her eyes. "Listen to me, I sound like you...being practical."

Rita studied the hallway. The section of hallway held only two doors. The first door belonged to a Mrs. Evelyn Ellsworth, whose name was on her door and had nodded to them in greeting through the open doorway; the second door belonged to Rusty. Rita's mind raced with questions. "I believe in being logical and practical at all times," Rita told Rhonda in a serious voice. "Critical thinking can't be ignored."

"And?" Rhonda asked. "So what?"

"So," Rita told her sister, "in this situation, logic points to helping an innocent man."

"How so?" Rhonda asked, leaning back against the wall and crossing her arms, peering at a painting of a wintry farm scene hanging against the colorful red wallpaper.

"You saw how he could barely walk without his cane. How could he even have the strength to complete a physical act like murder?" Rita stated.

Rhonda nodded. "You're right. In other words...we're not breaking the rules," Rhonda told her sister. "We're applying our own set of rational rules and logical work here."

Rita nodded her head. "In this case...yes."

Brad eased out of Rusty's room, closed the door, and walked over to Rita and Rhonda. "He's staring into thin air...lost inside of himself," he said in a miserable voice.

"Brad, who is Rusty's doctor?" Rhonda asked.

Brad took a puff of his pipe. "Doc Downing," he explained. "Downing makes a trip up here once a week and makes his rounds. When he's gone, Nurse Mae is in charge."

"So no outside doctors," Rhonda commented to Rita.

"That's good," Rita pointed out. "Fewer suspects. And we need to keep this investigation internal."

Rhonda nodded her head and focused on Brad. The poor man looked horrible and needed a distraction. "Brad, did you know about Beth and Noel?"

"No," Brad honestly answered. "Ladies, I haven't been up here in a couple of months." Brad looked down at his pipe. "I try to get up here and see Rusty as much as I can...but as you saw...he's getting worse. It's tough for me to see him like that."

"It is tough," Rita agreed. "A man who spent his life as a cop...tucked away from the world, forgotten...and forgetting himself."

"Very sad," Rhonda whispered.

"Maybe it's for the best." Brad raised his eyes. "The way the world is today...maybe it's better to forget what you were altogether and live in a daze until you die." Brad slapped out his pipe, shoved it into his pocket, and focused his eyes at Rusty's door. "Maybe it's better to forget instead of trying to remember...all remembering does is cause pain," he snapped and walked away.

Rita stepped next to Rhonda and watched Brad walk down the short hallway, turn a corner and vanish out of sight. "Poor man is really upset."

"Yes, he is," Rhonda agreed. "Can you blame him?"

"No, I can't," Rita replied and glanced in the other direction at the hallway that forked and led to what looked like a stairwell and another series of turns and twists. "Rhonda, Brad, and Mae were right about this mansion being designed like a maze. I've never seen so many hallways and doors in my life."

Rhonda locked her eyes on Rusty's door. "Which makes you wonder how a man who can barely remember his own name found his way to a woman's room on the other side of the third floor?"

"Exactly," Rita told her sister. "Lynn Hogan is on the west side of the third floor and Rusty's room is on the east side. In order to get to her room you have to go through a maze of hallways. Now, I could be wrong, but I don't think Rusty is capable of finding his way. I mean, I suppose it's possible. Rusty has been a resident here for a while and Mae did say he was good friends with Lynn and the poor man seems to have his lucid moments...but still...I just don't know."

"We have a lot of questions to ask and even more answers to track down," Rhonda told her sister, staring at Rusty's door with worried eyes. "Brad hasn't told anyone about the murder. Beth and Noel don't know. I'm worried if they do find out they'll call the outside world. We're going to have to work under the cloak of secrecy on this. Their hiring circumstances sure do look suspicious, but we can't afford to question them about it until the absolute last minute until we have evidence."

"You said it," Rita agreed. "Rusty Lowly is surely not a criminal. But he's depending on us to track down a killer, and we can't let the killer know he...or she...is being chased." Rita bit down on her lower lip and thought of the Pumpkin Festival. Oh, how she wanted to be back at the fairgrounds, eating a funnel cake, drinking hot apple cider, strolling around while resting her heart under a cool autumn sky. Instead she was trapped in a strange mansion attempting to save the life of a man who—as far as she knew—was being framed for the murder of an innocent woman. Then something occurred to her. "Rhonda?"

"Yes?"

"What if...by chance...Rusty did kill the wealthy woman...and he just can't remember doing it?" Rita asked in a scared voice. "Why? What could he have gained?"

Rhonda looked at her sister with uncertainty in her eyes. "I don't know," she answered and shook her head. "More importantly, if the unthinkable did take place...how could we get Rusty to remember what he did?"

"Let's just hope Rusty isn't the killer," Rita said and took Rhonda's hand. "We'll exhaust every alley there is to investigate before we investigate whether...Rusty might be the killer. Come on."

"To the kitchen?" Rhonda asked.

"To the kitchen," Rita nodded. "We can't tip our hand yet, but we do have two icebergs to meet."

Rhonda nodded, and then followed her sister down the short hallway and into the maze of hallways. As they worked their way through one hallway after another, Rhonda thought about Rusty Lowly. *How can we possibly rule that out?*

Downstairs in a large kitchen, two women with sour expressions labored in a cheerless silence. Beth slapped turkey onto a row of sandwiches on lunch plates, while Noel ladled into each bowl the tasteless soup steaming on the stovetop. The line of trays on the counter was labeled with each resident's name and dietary restrictions. When she reached Rusty's tray, Noel fished something out of the pocket of her apron. She opened the tiny capsule in her hand and poured a white powder into the man's soup and stirred it around and around until the powder vanished.

3

Rita entered the kitchen through a dim service hallway and immediately her nose alerted her to the overwhelming stench of rotting produce. Hunched over a worktable with her stringy hair escaping at the edges of a grease-stained white chef's cap, a woman listlessly slapped limp pieces of iceberg lettuce onto a row of sandwiches. The woman wasn't tall or short, fat or thin —she was utterly average and unremarkable, except for the air of poisonous malice that pervaded her entire being. "Are you Beth?" Rita asked.

Beth, who had not heard Rita enter the kitchen, spun around, startled, and nearly dropped her handful of lettuce on the floor. "I...didn't hear you come in," she said in a shaky voice and then quickly shook away her fear and slapped on a stern expression. "The kitchen is off limits to visitors."

Rita studied Beth. Narrowed, beady eyes peered out at her from under a mop of permed black hair that, Rita guessed, was supposed to be stylish but was perhaps ten years out of fashion. She studied eyes filled with suspicion and resentment and saw that Beth attempted to cloak her malice with a thin veneer of power. Under the woman's stained white apron she saw the ragged hems of black checkered uniform pants—the kind which chefs usually wore crisp and clean to convey their status in the kitchen—but here looked disgustingly faded. Not because she was a hard worker, obviously, but because she was sloppy and hated the work. Instead of power, Rita saw only stupidity and aggression.

"I was looking around," Rita explained, not responding to the woman's harsh comments. "I suppose I got lost again. Learning my way around this place is going to take some time."

Beth stared at Rita with eyes that grew more vicious by the second. "I'm not a tour guide," she snapped. "The kitchen is off limits. Now leave."

Rita felt frustration erupt in her heart. And because she wasn't officially a cop anymore, she allowed her anger to speak. "Sister," she snapped, pushing all rational thinking to the side, "you better watch your lip with me or I'll fatten it real quick. I've tangled with the best of them and I sure don't mind seeing who can mess up this kitchen more...you or me!"

Beth felt fear and shock rush into her chest. She was a woman who drew her bravery only from blunt fury and the kind of courage that comes from mindless mobs, or from a leader she could shield herself behind. But when forced to stand alone—forced to face a courageous person who was not cowed by simple threats—Beth's cowardice revealed its true colors. "Get out of the kitchen...before I call the head nurse," she stuttered, hunching over the table like a kicked dog.

"I have every right to be in this kitchen," Rita explained and took a step toward Beth. Beth quickly retreated further behind the kitchen table. "My sister and I have been hired as security."

"Security?" Beth asked.

Rita nodded.

"I'm aware of that," Beth dared to answer in a snotty voice, grasping for control even though her words left her mouth shaky and uncertain.

"Then you're aware that the Street Riders could be coming into town."

"Street Riders?" Beth asked, stopping in her tracks.

Rita nodded her head and dived into the cover story she and Rhonda had created and passed by Brad and Mae; it was vital that they possessed an undercover identity that would be believable without throwing suspicion into their corner. The idea of two security guards felt promising, just as long as the story about a gang of car thieves passed. "The Street Riders are a gang of car thieves that target large events...concerts...festivals," Rita explained. "Last week they hit a city in Tennessee pretty hard and got away with over fifteen vehicles. State officials contacted the local sheriff and warned him that the gang might target the Pumpkin Festival."

"What does that have to with coming up here?" Beth asked in a suspicious tone. "No car thief is going to try to steal a car this far out."

"Word is," Rita continued and braced herself against the countertop casually, "the guy in charge of the Street Riders knows someone right here at this home." Rita looked around, pretending to make sure no one was listening, "He knows the residents have a lot of cars stored on the property…nice cars. Old people take good care of their cars, you know. But sometimes they forget to lock them, see? So my sister and I are undercover," she whispered. "We believe it's possible that the Street Riders may show up here."

Beth stared at Rita in disbelief. "You're...kidding me, right?" she asked in a cynical voice.

"No, I'm not," Rita assured Beth. "A car has already been stolen from the fairgrounds. Now, that car could have been taken by anyone, but," she said in a careful voice, "I don't think it's a coincidence that a car was stolen in a town only a couple of hours away from place the Street Riders hit last week." Rita looked around again. "It's very possible that the guy running the gang will show up here. My job is to talk to the residents...ask some questions, you know?" Rita focused back on Beth. "Your job is to keep your mouth shut. Is that clear?"

"Who...who do you think you are?" Beth asked in a shaky voice. "You can't just order me around. My manager will—"

Rita reached down into the front pocket of her coat and pulled out the deputy badge that Brad had given her on the ride up to the retirement home. "I'm a cop, got it?" she snapped. "And if you want to play nice, keep your mouth shut. If you want to end up in jail...well, run your mouth and see what happens," she warned Beth. "I'm starting to think some of the staff around here might not be cooperative with our undercover operation, and if so, we've been deputized to take them in for questioning…if you don't want that to happen, I suggest you play nice." She gave Beth a meaningful look. "We are here to catch a gang of car thieves. If you step in our way I'll slap a pair of handcuffs on you so fast you won't be able to blink. Is that clear, sister?"

Fear warred with defiance on Beth's face. She despised most people. She despised cops especially—and everything they stood for. She had also never met a situation she could not get out of with a few cruel words. She clawed for one last power grab, sneering at Rita, "I don't like being...threatened."

"It's not a threat, it's a promise," Rita said simply. "I'm simply making it clear that I have a job to do and that you better stand clear." Rita looked away from Beth, unable to bear the sight of the woman any longer, and studied the kitchen.

The kitchen was spacious and although it clearly was not getting cleaned very well under the new chef and nutritionist, the cabinets were white with red knobs, and the floor was red and white checkered tile, continuing the theme of the whole house. "Nice," she said and walked over to a door. The door was unlocked and she opened it, realizing it led directly outside. "I want this door kept locked at all times," she ordered and quickly activated the deadbolt.

"That's against fire code."

Rita shot Beth a look and pointed over to the obvious Fire Exit sign posted over the other doorway leading to the back hallway. Beth quickly lowered her eyes. "Locked at all times, is that clear?"

"I'll...keep the door locked," Beth assured Rita and looked uncomfortable. "Look, how much longer you gonna ask questions? Noel is serving trays...I have work to do."

Rita looked back at Beth. "How long have you been working here?" she asked.

"Couple of months. Why?"

"Where are you from?" Rita asked.

"Am I under arrest?" Beth shot back. "I know my rights. I don't have to answer any questions—"

"Give your mouth a break," Rita snapped. "I'm just asking you some questions. Would you rather I run your background and find out that way? Fine by me."

Beth swallowed. "Run my background...that's illegal."

"Not if you're obstructing an investigation, giving me probable cause to believe you're tied to the Street Riders," Rita informed Beth and slowly folded her arms. "You're a new employee and you don't exactly look like this is your dream job. Rita eyed Beth with cold calculation. "I'm not stupid, sister."

"Now wait a minute," Beth objected, "I don't even know who the Street Riders are. There's no proof, you can't just accuse me of—"

"I'm not accusing you of anything," Rita interrupted Beth in a calmer tone of voice. "All I'm pointing out is that I can run your background whether you like it not. And," Rita said, fully embracing the bad cop role in order to shake Beth up, "maybe I already have."

Beth swallowed again. Rita had her arm twisted and there was nothing she could do about it. "Look," she said, "I've been working here for a couple of months. I'm from Woodstock, Georgia. I moved to Atlanta years ago...went to a culinary school...and decided to become a medical chef, okay? Are you happy?"

"Married? Boyfriend?"

Beth lowered her eyes. "No."

"Family?"

Beth swallowed again and looked toward the kitchen door. If only Noel was in the kitchen...but Noel was serving the food trays. "Noel, the nutritionist, she's my...sister," Beth told Rita with obvious reluctance. Noel had warned Beth to keep her mouth shut and not speak to anyone, and now was she spilling her life history to this pushy cop.

Rita stared at Beth's cold face—a face scarred with years of suspicion and anger and malice aimed at mankind. It was a wonder the residents' food didn't taste bitter every day, with this woman cooking. "My sister is talking to Noel as we speak," Rita informed Beth.

Beth yanked her head up. "She is?" she asked in an alarmed voice.

"Yes," Rita nodded, reading fear in Beth's eyes. As she stared into Beth's eyes an idea struck her mind. "Maybe I can solve this case right here and now," she whispered and quickly narrowed her eyes at Beth. "Cost lots of money to live here, doesn't it?" she asked. "People living here aren't poor, are they?"

"I...I wouldn't know," Beth said, becoming more nervous and unhinged by the second. She jerked her eyes at the back door and began wondering how long it would take her to throw the deadbolt open, race to her car, and escape. But then Noel entered the kitchen striding with anger and purpose. "Noel!" Beth shouted to warn her, with her eyes darting over at Rita.

"Don't say a word to these cops unless our lawyer is present," Noel yelled at Beth and threw a hard finger at Rita. "I know our rights!"

Rita spotted Rhonda walk in behind Noel. Rhonda rolled her eyes in a way that let Rita know that Noel was going to be a real difficult case. "Just don't get in our way," Rita snapped at Noel, sticking with her tough cop voice. She quickly scanned Noel and was surprised that she was so unlike her friend; instead of a uniform greasy with stains, Noel wore a long brown and green floral dress with vintage lace details down the sides. The dress had clearly seen better days. "Shouldn't you be wearing an apron?"

Noel dropped her eyes down to her flower child dress and her worn leather hippie sandals. "We know our rights," she repeated, pulling her long brown hair tighter into its ponytail. "Don't need you nosing around in our business, city girl," she sneered. Like Beth, Noel thrived on petty power.

Rita looked at Rhonda. Rhonda rolled her eyes again. "I told her she looks like nineteen-sixties reject and she got mad. Go figure."

"You insulted me," Noel hissed, playing the victim.

Rhonda, who had decided to play the good cop, grinned. "Honey, with that outfit...how could I not?" she asked. "I'm sorry, I'm just genuinely concerned. I didn't mean to insult you. I just meant you look like you could use a mother's touch...I know my mama would never let me walk out of the house looking like something dug up out of the rag bin in the back of the barn."

"See? See?" Noel complained to Rita, incensed.

Rita fought back a grin. Rhonda was doing great. Mae has warned them that Noel was the ringleader and that Beth was a follower. After tossing a coin, Rita won the right to go after Beth first, and Rhonda won Noel. Mae also suggested that a bad-cop approach would work especially well with Beth, who wouldn't know how to react while the ringleader Noel was on her rounds delivering the food trays. Rhonda, in the meantime, annoyed Noel and picked at her mind like a woodpecker attacking a sour tree. Rita put on a false air of admonishment. "Rhonda, we're here on official business. Quit telling stories and trying to mother them. They're grown workers, after all."

Rhonda walked over to the kitchen counter, studied the bread left in a sloppy pile by the sandwiches, and then turned to face Noel. Noel made her cringe all over. The woman's expression was uglier than a trail of slime. Beth, she quickly noticed, wasn't too far behind. "Look, ladies," she said, "we're here to catch the Street Riders, okay? The leader might pay us a visit and when we catch him we can take down his entire gang. It's that simple. But first we need to know all about you. I mean, come on, it is a little...interesting...that you two started to work here right around the same time the Street Riders were known to be on the move."

"I've already told you," Noel snapped, "we don't know who these Street Riders are. My friend and I were hired because there were two open positions, simple as that." Noel stepped closer to Beth. "I can show you my credentials and so can Beth."

Rhonda shrugged her shoulders. "Maybe later," she said and tossed a thumb at a white refrigerator. "I'm hungry. Anything in the fridge?"

"Food's for residents only," Beth snapped, a little more courageous now that Noel was back at her side. "Stay out."

Rita shot a hard look at Beth. "Watch that the attitude," she warned. Beth flinched. "Come on Rhonda," she said, "these two are clearly a waste of our time. They aren't smart enough to steal a breadcrumb, let alone help a gang of car thieves. We better get to talking to the guests."

Rhonda looked at Beth and Noel and studied their eyes. It was clear to her that the two women had bought the fake story hook, line, and sinker. "Pity we're stuck out here on this job," she mused as they left. "I'd rather be at the Pumpkin Festival. I saw a really cute rug that would go perfect in front of the fireplace. You know, the blue and brown one with the bear on it?"

Rita picked up on her sister's tactic. "I already told you to forget about that ugly rug."

"Ugly?" Rhonda asked in an insulted tone and threw her hands up. "Did you hear that?" she asked.

"Oh, good grief," Rita complained, "we're trying to run down a car thief and you're worried about a rug." Rita turned, shaking her head, and stormed out of the kitchen.

"My, she's touchy today," Rhonda said and placed her hands on her hips stubbornly. "I guess I should go talk to her. Uh, you ladies...carry on...with what you were doing, okay? If we have any more questions we'll let you know." And with those words Rhonda hurried after Rita, leaving Beth and Noel very confused and very on edge.

Rita worked her way up to the third floor with Rhonda, struggling through one confusing hallway after the next. Each hallway's decorations reflected the red and white color scheme of a peppermint candy cane—a cozy look, but very annoying when trying to navigate a confusing building. "Isn't this the same suit of armor we just saw? Michael Stonewell must have been a very eccentric person," Rita sighed as she turned around. "We need to go back to the stairwell...again. Where's that map we were promised?"

Rhonda grinned. Sure, getting lost was annoying but kinda fun. "We sure had those two in the kitchen confused, didn't we?"

Rita stopped, stared at the red and white striped wallpaper hung with yet another row of charming paintings of snowy town scenes. "I'm relieved they bought our story," she pointed out. "I'm confident those two women believe the Street Riders story. Also, guess what Mae doesn't know… they're sisters."

"Really? Maybe that should come as no surprise. They're certainly similar enough in their attitudes…anyway, I'm grateful Mae has not told them that Lynn Hogan died this morning," Rhonda added. "Mae told Noel that the lady wasn't feeling well and was not to be disturbed. Noel bought the story and left the lunch tray outside her room."

"You were with Mae?" Rita asked.

"I walked by just in the nick of time," Rhonda explained and ran her finger over the red and white wallpaper covering the hallway.

Rita shifted her attention to a closed door. "Lucky timing pays off," she said and carefully eased it open. "A storeroom," she said.

Rhonda stepped up behind Rita, peered into a dimly lit room lined with boxes, spotted an oval window covered with a simple green drape, and nodded her head. "Seems to be."

Rita walked into the room and went over to a pile of boxes. "Let's see what's inside of these boxes."

"Well...usually we would need a search warrant," Rhonda teased her sister, "but since we're no longer on the payroll...why not?" Rhonda hurried over to a box and opened the lid. "Old books in this box. What do you have?"

Rita opened a box and peered inside. "Files," she said. Rhonda turned around, watched her sister extract a manila folder, and open it. "Seems to be files on residents who lived here in the past," she explained. "Each one has a date of death stamped at the top."

Rhonda walked over to Rita and studied the open file. "Charlie Keatington...age ninety-one...resident for eight years...died four years ago. This form indicates he died of natural causes."

Rita looked at Rhonda. "Poor guy. I don't think these files will help us, Rhonda. I wish we knew more about Miss Katherine," she said, closed the file, tossed it back into the box, and looked around the room. "Mae said Katherine was responsible for the candy cane designs everywhere... she had a childlike heart. I wonder if her daughter is truly following in her footsteps."

Rhonda walked over to the oval window, pulled back the green drape, and looked down at a beautiful cast iron bench below, nestled in a flower garden that simply took her breath away. "I don't think Kathy Stein is on the wrong side of the law, Rita."

"I know." Rita walked to the window and looked out. "I only wish I knew more about the woman, on a personal level," she explained. She looked around at the ornately decorated room; even though it was simply used for storage she could see the details around the windows and the doorway. "What would make a woman buy this mansion...turn it into a retirement home...and decorate every twisting, turning little corridor like a candy cane? Why did Miss Katherine live here? Why did she have her daughter here? I'm very curious to know who Katherine Stein truly was." Rita sighed. "And on another level, on an investigative level—"

"You want to know exactly who her daughter Kathy Stein really is," Rhonda finished for sister. "Me too. That whole business about Kathy Stein donating all the extra profits to a food charity doesn't sit right in my gut. I think Mae honestly believes that, but I don't. I don't think Brad does, either."

Rita watched fall colored leaves dance in the wind, land in a nearby stream flowing over sleepy rocks, and nodded her head. "I don't believe that story, either," she agreed. "Rhonda, we need to get in touch with Ollie Rooney and Patty Olson."

"Mae said Ollie and Patty didn't leave forwarding addresses or phone numbers," Rhonda pointed out, wistfully keeping her eyes on the beautiful day. "Tracking them down will take some time."

Rita bit down on her lower lip. "I know." Tracking down two people who might have been scared away from a job they once loved and adored was going to be tough. "Brad is going to have to go back into town and start searching the database for us."

"Yeah, that is what I was thinking," Rhonda agreed. "Brad sure isn't going to like leaving Rusty."

"What choice does he have?" Rita asked. "Mae said that Kathy sent Beth and Noel here the very day Ollie Rooney and Patty Olson quit. That's no coincidence." Rita walked back out into the hallway. Rhonda followed. "Two things are going through my mind."

Rhonda closed the door to the storage room. "I think I know what those two things are," she said. "Either Kathy Stein is corrupt, pocketing the profits and maybe she's even after Lynn Hogan's money…or she's being held hostage by some other secret tied to this mansion, something that led her to manipulate the employees like that, firing some and hiring others."

Rhonda nodded her head. "We could be wrong, of course...and maybe in time we'll have to adjust our theories, but for now—"

"All we have are two wheels instead of four," Rhonda told her sister. She looked down the short hallway. "We better try again," she said and got her legs moving. Rita slowly followed and she turned to look at her. "Rita?"

"Yes?"

"Mae locked the walk-in freezer and told Beth and Noel it was on the blink, right?" Rhonda asked.

"Yes, that's what Mae told them. I didn't focus too much on the lock," Rita replied. "My attention was on Beth."

Rhonda stopped walking, turned, and looked at her twin sister with curious eyes. "I hate to admit this," she said, lowering her voice down to a whisper, "but what if Mae is somehow involved? It appears that she is an honest and kind woman, but...what if?"

"I thought about that," Rita confessed, "but I keep going back to what Brad told us." Rita looked past Rhonda, made sure the coast was clear, and then went on. "Brad said he and Mae carried Lynn Hogan's body into the walk-in freezer before Beth and Noel arrived for work. He watched Mae put the padlock on the freezer door. Mae gave Brad the key to the padlock. If Mae was involved, I don't think she would have reported the murder right to him and cooperated with us."

Rhonda rubbed her chin. "I know the evidence points to Mae being in the clear, but...it was the way she talked to Noel." Rhonda shook her head. "Noel was very harsh with me but she seemed...easier with Mae when we saw her in the corridor. Not by much...but a little. Mae seemed stern with Noel, but not in a way that sat well in my gut."

"Why didn't you say this before?"

"Because a part of me still wants to believe that people are good, no matter my fears to the contrary," Rhonda confessed in a miserable voice. "And maybe I am wrong...I hope I'm wrong. I hope Mae is as innocent as a newborn rabbit...or deer...or whatever woodland creature you want to compare her to." Rhonda sighed. "Rita, if Mae is involved it will break my heart...that's why I kept it to myself at first. But we are cops at heart...we follow the clues…and I needed you to know."

Rita studied the pain in her sister's eyes. "I can see that it hurts you to tell me. I'm sorry."

"Let's just hope I'm wrong," Rhonda responded and patted Rita's hand. "We better get our legs working or we're never going to find our way back to Mae's office." Rita hesitated. "What is it?"

"If Mae is involved...then Beth and Noel will know the truth," Rita explained in a worried voice. "Beth was getting ready to run. I read her eyes and face as clear as day. But as soon as Noel entered the kitchen, she calmed down." Rita studied the hallway, struggling to put her thoughts into words. "Noel is a hard woman full of cruel intentions. The sight of her makes me feel disgusted. Mae told us both Noel and Beth are cold as ice...so why hasn't Mae fired them? Why hasn't she complained to Kathy Stein and insisted a new chef and nutritionist be hired?"

"I was wondering when you were going to toss that question at me." Rhonda glanced back over her shoulder, more out of habit than concern, and then continued. "That's another thing that concerned me while I watched her talking with Noel." Rhonda looked Rita in her eyes. "I know Beth and Noel bought the whole Street Rider story, but Mae sure put a lot of beans into the pot when we were coming up with the story."

"Are you saying you went along with the story in order to deceive Mae?"

"I sure did," Rhonda nodded her head. "Now, before you get all upset with me," she begged Rita, "please know that I didn't tell you because, deep down, I still want to believe Mae is innocent...and maybe she is. I don't want to chance ruining our whole plan by throwing suspicion on Mae when I don't have a shred of evidence yet. I figured it was better to run with the plan and see what happened." Rhonda made a pained face. "You're mad at me, aren't you?"

"No, no, I'm not mad," Rita quickly replied. "Rhonda, I guess I would have done the same thing. You were smart in keeping your mouth shut." Rita patted Rhonda's shoulder. "You've always been able to read people better than me, sis. That's what makes us a great team. You have your talents and I have mine."

Relief washed through Rhonda. "Whew, for a minute there I thought I was going to have kitchen duty for an entire month."

"You still might," Rita tried to joke but failed. "Sometimes I wish I could be like you, Rhonda. You're always able to toss a joke into the air, laugh at silly things. Sometimes I hate being so practical about things." Rita looked down at her soft hands. "Sometimes I fear that I'm nothing but a bore."

"Oh, that's not true," Rhonda assured her sister. "Rita, you may not be a born comedian, but you're not a boring woman. Your practical streak has saved our bacon more times than I can count. Why, there are times when I would give my right arm to be able to think the way you do."

"You mean join me in the world of black and white account books and boring habits?"

"No, silly," Rhonda said and took Rita's hands. "Take the cabin for example."

"Okay."

"I didn't want the cabin, did I?" Rhonda asked. "Not at first, anyway."

"No, you wanted to buy the house up on Candy Cane Peak."

"Because of the view," Rhonda agreed. "Oh, I was set on buying that house just for the view. I wasn't thinking very practical, let me tell you. You had to remind me that the drive from Candy Cane Peak into town was over twenty miles and that we would need to buy a four-wheel drive just to get home in a light snowfall. On top of that, you had to remind me that no amount of lovely sunsets or sunrises would save us from a basement that leaked, the roof that needed to be replaced, and that whole southern wall that was suffering from wood rot so bad you could use the back door as a pillow!"

Rita finally let out a small chuckle. "It's true, you were blind to all of that. We would have spent more money repairing that house than we ended up spending on our whole cute, little cabin."

"Exactly," Rhonda pointed out. "You see, I was thinking with my emotions but you remained...well, practical. And by doing so you saved us a lot of headaches and money. In time, we were able to find a lovely cabin that we both adore."

"And within our financial limits," Rita agreed proudly. It was satisfying to remember how it had all worked out.

There were consolations to being the practical sister, after all.

Rhonda smiled. "Rita, we think differently at times, but our minds always complement each other, whether in the bakery or as cops...my mind running this way, your mind running that way. We always meet in the middle, or manage to get things done the best way we can. I guess what I'm trying to say is that you're my better half and I'm your better half and if we didn't have each other, why, we wouldn't be complete."

Rita looked into her sister's caring eyes and smiled. "You do have a way of making a gal feel better."

"Aw, shucks," Rhonda said in a silly western drawl, "'twasn't nothin'. That's what twin sisters are for, pardner."

Rita rolled her eyes. "Now that I would never do...not in public anyway."

Rhonda laughed. "I would take a video of you if you tried and send it to Mom and Dad."

"Dad would fall out of his recliner," Rita laughed back. "I'm the daughter who checks the old tax returns just for the fun of it. Just like he taught me. He might lose it."

"Yeah," Rhonda said and made a pained face, "Dad doesn't really let himself relax very much, does he? Poor guy thinks watching documentaries on how ants built an ant hill is fun."

"Last time we were there, he watched paint dry in the garage. Literally," Rita said and let out a sympathetic laugh. "Poor Mom, every time she jokes with Dad he gives her one of his looks."

"I know," Rhonda moaned. "Remember when she put a fake spider under his newspaper at the breakfast table?"

"How can I forget," Rita laughed. "Dad picked up his newspaper, picked up the spider, handed it to mom, and said in his most boring voice: "Your attempt to scare me is not amusing. This spider is clearly fake. Now, where is my coffee…" Rita suddenly stopped laughing. Her face went pale. "Oh my...am I that bad, Rhonda?"

Rhonda grimaced. "Well, when I try to pull a joke on you...you kinda turn into Dad. But not all the time...just when I..." Rhonda lowered her eyes. "You just don't like to have jokes played on you, that's all."

"See? I told you. It's because I don't have a sense of humor," Rita nearly cried. "Down in the kitchen I handled Beth the way I would handle a dog on a leash...good enough for a cop…but I couldn't tell a joke if my life depended on it. Can't take a joke, either. No wonder I'm not married."

"Oh dear," Rhonda whispered, realizing that she now had more than a murder case on her hands: she had an upset sister, which was far worse. They didn't have time for this conversation, however. "Come on, sis, no time to solve that particular issue right now. We better go find Brad and

Mae." Rita nodded her head and glumly walked off with Rhonda.

As they headed down the corridor, hesitantly looking for the stairs, Rusty sat alone at his little table and uncovered the lunch tray. Was it lunch already? He couldn't seem to remember anymore, but he was hungry. The sandwich was good but the soup tasted a bit...strange. Of course, after Rusty ate a few more bites he forgot all about the strange taste.

4

Nurse Mae looked up when Rita and Rhonda entered her office. "Sheriff and I were getting worried," she said.

Rita closed the door and focused on Mae, who sat behind a humble wooden desk with a simple white office phone, a clipboard from her nursing rounds, and a few folders and invoices. She noticed a drawing of some kind. "Is that the diagram?" she asked.

"To the best of my memory," Mae nodded.

"Boy, do we need this," said Rita, looking it over eagerly.

Rhonda stepped up to Brad, who was leaning against a wooden filing cabinet. Brad was filling his pipe from the small pouch he kept in his breast pocket, tapping cherry tobacco into the bowl. "We need you to go back into town," she said in a cop voice.

Brad lowered his pipe in surprise. "I'm not leaving Rusty."

"We need to you try and locate Ollie Rooney and Patty Olson," Rita told Brad.

Nurse Mae stood up. "What for?" she asked.

"Follow-up questions," Rita explained without elaborating. She scanned the office, pretending to be bored. The office walls were painted in a soft brown, with a worn hardwood floor and a popcorn ceiling. A few simple nature paintings hung about, but nothing grand. All in all, the office was bland and nothing like the cheerily decorated floors they had been wandering around in. "Mae, Rhonda, and I are confident that Beth and Noel bought our story. That's good. But we still have a lot of paths to investigate."

"We need answers," Rhonda jumped in. "I'm sure you can understand that," she finished and carefully read Mae's eyes. "You look worried…is something wrong?"

"No...well, maybe," Mae confessed. "Ollie and Patty..." She paused.

"What about them?" Brad asked. "You could save me a trip into town if you know where they are."

"Ollie and Patty—" Mae lost her nerve again and fiddled with the clipboard in front of her.

Brad stuffed his pipe into his front pants pocket. "Mae, whatever it is, I can run their names through the system and find it out. Just tell us."

"That's what worries me," Mae blurted out. "You see, Ollie and Patty...oh, they worked for cheap for a reason, Brad," she confessed in a miserable voice. "Ollie, as sweet and caring as he was...the man was a heavy drinker. He never took a sip on duty, of course, but in his spare time…" Mae shook her head. "You can figure it out."

"I guess we can," Rhonda nodded.

Mae picked up a pen and began fiddling with it. "Ollie had been arrested a few times for drinking and driving in the past. He sobered up long enough to attend culinary school and decided to become a medical chef. He went through the proper schooling, received the right training, and became certified, all the right steps, but…"

"But no one would hire him because of his record, right?" Rhonda asked.

Mae looked up. "Exactly," she said with a sigh. She turned to adjust a white curtain near her desk, opening to an oval window that looked out upon the river sparkling in the autumn sunshine. "Chefs make good money...and medical chefs make a little bit more. Plus the healthcare industry offers security. Restaurants go out of business every day, but hospitals are always open. Ollie took the safe route, but there wasn't a hospital in the state that would touch him. For liability reasons, you see."

Rita and Rhonda both looked at each other. Rita nodded her head. Rhonda nodded back. "Mae, how did Kathy Stein come to hire Ollie Rooney? Why did she make an exception for him?"

Mae watched the river dance through a stand of trees. "Let me explain something first. The retirement home never had a nutritionist in the old days," she explained. "Joan Bateman was the cook here for years. Miss Katherine and Joan were the very best of friends." Mae kept her eyes on the river. "After Miss Katherine died, Joan stayed on for a while longer...longer than I expected, to be honest. Joan was already in her seventies at the time but somehow kept up with her kitchen duties."

"What happened to her?" Rita asked.

"The state came in and started changing all the rules after a resident, Remy Cunningham, had a medical scare. Mr. Cunningham's blood pressure was through the roof and his blood sugar was awful." Mae shook her head. "Mr. Cunningham's doctor reported us to the state and soon after, this fancy, snotty woman comes barging in wearing one of those shiny business suits, asking nosy questions, ordering me around like I was trash." Mae made a sour face. "I was required to hire a medical chef and a nutritionist that would adhere to each patient's nutritional needs or be shut down."

"I guess that's...reasonable," Rhonda said.

Mae sighed. "I suppose," she agreed. "Joan was getting old...and a tad forgetful. Joan would never deliberately cook anything that would hurt a resident. But maybe she cut corners here and there. She put love into her cooking." Mae finally turned around and looked at the others. "Joan couldn't keep up with the state's new rules. She simply packed her bags, hugged me goodbye, and took a bus to

Alabama where her sister lives. I've never heard from her since."

"How long after Joan left did Kathy Stein hire Ollie?" Rhonda began to ask.

"I do the hiring, actually," Mae corrected Rhonda. "I hire the groundskeepers, the gardeners, and the inside help. Or I used to, anyway. That's was why it was so strange for Kathy to send me Beth and Noel..."

Rhonda studied Mae. Something wasn't quite right. "Okay, but we'll come back to that. First let's focus on Ollie," she said. "How long was it before you hired Ollie?"

Mae frowned. "I needed a cook and a nutritionist immediately...but I couldn't pay the salaries the market demanded. Joan worked for cheap because she lived in the gardener's old house at the back of the property, and...she also took her pay in cash, under the table." Mae looked at Brad with shameful eyes. "Katherine always paid Joan cash...I couldn't change the rules. But I promise that Ollie and Patty's salaries were legal."

Brad shrugged his shoulders. "Ain't none of my business how Joan was paid just as long as she wasn't a criminal. I ain't going to call up the IRS on you, Mae. Besides, that's long past, and Miss Katherine is long dead now."

Mae gave Brad a look of gratitude. "Thank you," she said. Brad shrugged his shoulders again.

"Okay, Mae," Rhonda said, "how did you hire Ollie?"

"I put an ad in with the Georgia Department of Labor. Ollie, along with about thirty other people, replied. Each person wanted more money than we could pay...Ollie was the cheapest and willing to start right away. He was already suited up in his apron and washing his hands in the kitchen when his background check came in. I had to have background checks on all new employees...another rule from the snotty woman..." Mae sighed again. "I talked to him about his past and told him I could only offer him a cheaper salary for the week, as a sort of probationary period. I know it was probably wrong, but Ollie never did a single thing to break our faith in him and I continued to keep him on...but I still feel bad to this day. I kept him at that lower salary for the whole time and he never complained. I guess he knew he wouldn't get anything else." Mae looked at Brad. "According to the snotty woman who set down the new rules, I wasn't supposed to hire anyone with a criminal history. I could have been shut down for hiring Ollie."

"Like I said, I ain't interested in digging up old skeletons," Brad told Mae in a voice that let her know her minor infractions were not what they were trying to unfold.

"Why was money a problem in the first place?" Rita asked Mae. "You said Kathy Stein donates any money left over from this home to a food charity. Why didn't she just increase the salary budget so you could hire someone without a criminal history?"

Mae walked back to her desk, took a piece of peppermint candy out of a white candy dish, and opened it. "I know what I told you about the donations," she said in an upset voice. "I told you what I did because I wanted to protect Kathy. It's my...duty to protect my boss, right? I need my job. I figured I could stop you from asking questions if I...told that little lie." Mae looked at Rita and Rhonda. "You girls didn't believe me anyway. I saw your eyes."

"No, we didn't," Rita confessed.

"Sorry," Rhonda added, "but your lie didn't hold water."

"I was worried about that," Mae said and put the piece of peppermint candy in her mouth. "As you can both see, there are no grounds workers here today, no staff, no gardeners...just me." Mae walked back to the window. "When Miss Katherine was alive she was able to have a full-time staff...but as she grew closer and closer to death, Kathy took over the finances..." Mae gazed at the river again. "The money seemed to grow very thin."

"We're all ears," Rita assured Mae.

Mae worked on the piece of peppermint candy in her mouth as the leaves played in the cool wind outside. Oh, how she wanted to be at the pumpkin festival instead of trapped inside of a nightmare. "You saw how I was talking with Noel," she told Rhonda. "Yes, you saw. I read your face."

Rhonda glanced at Rita. Mae was smarter than she appeared. "Yes, I saw...and I began wondering a whole lot of things, too."

"Perhaps you began to question my loyalties, when you saw that?" Mae asked.

"Yes."

Mae shook her head. "I can't stand Noel and Beth," she gritted out through her teeth. "I only pretend to tolerate Noel because I fear her."

"Why?" Rita asked. She looked toward Brad and saw him pull his pipe back out. Brad wasn't interested in talking. All the man was interested in doing was listening—for the time being.

Mae hugged her arms. "The paperwork Kathy Stein sent me is legitimate, or so it appears. Kathy isn't interested in having the state pay us another visit. But somehow I feel the two women are frauds...sent here to...to...I just don't know! I can't bring myself to voice what's really screaming inside of my heart."

"Please, talk to us, Mae," Rhonda pleaded, "because—"

"You think I'm involved with Lynn Hogan's murder," Mae told Rhonda with misery in her voice.

"Yes," Rhonda confessed. "Please, Mae, prove me wrong, because I don't want to believe that a woman like yourself can be involved with the two ugly rats downstairs in the kitchen."

Mae stood silent for a minute. When she spoke her voice came out shaky. "Kathy...it has to be Kathy," she whispered miserably. "Mrs. Hogan wasn't loaded with diamonds, but her millions aren't anything to sneeze at, either." Mae slowly turned to face Rita and Rhonda. "Kathy controls the money," she confessed. "And she sent me Beth and Noel. It has to be her, right? I just can't fathom it…but like I said, Kathy controls all the business accounts and mails out employee checks and tells me how much money I can spend on expenses, which isn't much."

"How are the grounds so well kept?" Rita asked. "I'm sure—"

"Volunteers," Mae explained. "Local historical preservation society folks take care of the special flower gardens sometimes, but it's mainly the high school kids that come here twice a month. All I know is there's some kind of program that earns them credit for college. I'm not exactly sure how that works. Busloads of kids show up from different schools around the state and break their backs for free. They're like an army with their rakes and shovels and leaf blowers and whatnot. How Kathy managed to finagle free labor is beyond me," Mae sighed. "The kids also deep clean...the kind of stuff I simply can't do…they vacuum, mop, wash the windows, help with the laundry. I'm grateful for them, but...I feel so guilty."

Rita sat down in a wooden chair in front of Mae's desk. She decided to take a different tack. "Mae, let's go back a second. What can you tell us about Patty Olson?" she asked. "We know about Ollie, but what about Patty Olson?"

Rhonda fiddled with an unwrapped piece of peppermint from the candy dish and waited for Mae to answer. She drew in a deep breath of cherry tobacco, looked at Brad, saw the man intently focused on Mae, and then focused back on the nurse.

"Patty was a close friend of Ollie's," Mae explained. "Ollie and Patty applied for jobs at some hospital on the same day and met, years ago. Ollie, charming and funny as he was, started to date Patty but their romance fell apart a little. They were more close friends by the time they came here. I guess Ollie found out that Patty had been divorced four times...guess he wasn't interested in being number five. For her part, she wasn't happy about his alcoholism." Mae sighed. "Patty was a recovering alcoholic. She had stayed on the right side of the law, but she had been fired from three different locations for coming to work...sauced. Maybe I shouldn't have hired Patty, but like Ollie...she agreed to work cheap. They were sort of a package deal." Mae looked at Brad. Brad shrugged his shoulders again. "Ollie and Patty were the best people," she said with genuine conviction. "I wish you could have met them. Patty even tried to help Ollie quit drinking...and Ollie, in time, maybe he would have kicked the bottle, too. But now they're both gone and if you go chasing after them, stirring up what happened long ago...whatever life they might have now, if any, could go down the tubes quickly."

"You said Ollie went to Maine and Patty went west?" Rita asked.

"Oh, that's what they claimed, but I know better," Mae explained. "Ollie could barely deal with the cold winters here in Clovedale Falls, let alone the frigid northern winters he grew up with in Maine. And Patty's mother is over ninety-five years old and lives in one of the best nursing homes in Arizona. Patty's brother lives near there and visits his mother often, pays the bill for any extras she might need. He has made it clear on several occasions that he doesn't want his sister around." Mae looked at Rita and Rhonda. "I think Ollie and Patty left the state of Georgia, but not headed for where they claimed. And I don't think it was a coincidence, either. I think...they were scared off."

"By your boss, Kathy?" Rhonda asked.

"You tell me what it looks like," Mae answered. She turned back to the window. "Ollie and Patty leave, two dreadful women show up in their places...millionaire Lynn Hogan is found dead...what am I supposed to believe?" Mae shivered all over. "I made a promise to Miss Katherine to remain steadfast at my work here, take care of this home the way she would have liked it...take care of the residents...and watch over her daughter and her legacy. But I fear the time is coming when I might be forced to leave myself."

"Don't say that," Brad finally spoke. He walked over to Mae. "You've been here for years, Mae. This place is your home and always will be. Yeah, a murder has taken place, but you better believe I'm breaking a whole bunch of rules right now so we can find out what's going on and who really killed Mrs. Hogan. And I won't let Kathy Stein sweep anything under the rug, or scare off any more staff, if she really has anything to do with this."

Mae looked into Brad's kind face. "Do you really believe I could keep this place going without Kathy running interference with the state regulations people? The state will shut me down, Sheriff," she said in a pitiful voice. "And even if they don't, once word of the murder gets onto the front page of every paper in Georgia, no one will ever darken our door again. Can you imagine settling dear old grandma and grandpa in a retirement home where a murder took place?" Her eyes were wide with horror and despair. "The money will dry up...the free labor Kathy has arranged will come to an end. This home will fall into ruins within a decade and finally be condemned once and for all."

"Hey," Brad said and put a caring hand on Mae's shoulder, "don't talk like that. Everything is going to be fine."

"That's what people say in the movies, Sheriff. This is real life," Mae told Brad and pointed toward the office door. "There is a dead body in the walk-in freezer downstairs...a dead body, Brad! I was almost shut down for letting Joan put too much salt and sugar in the food. What do you think the state is going to do to me when they find out I was hiding a dead body in my kitchen? Or that I hired Beth and Noel, who just may have stabbed Lynn to death this morning?" Mae hid her face in her hands.

Rita and Rhonda glanced at each other. It seemed to them that Mae had more worries on her stressed mind than they realized. But at least she didn't seem to be involved in the murder of Lynn Hogan; or so they hoped.

LET'S BAKE A DEAL

The quiet of the office shattered with the sound of footsteps thundering toward Nurse Mae's office, and the door was flung open. Clutching her purse, Noel stormed into Mae's office. "We quit!" she yelled at Mae and pointed at Rita and Rhonda. "Beth and I are not going to stand around and be punching bags for this so-called... security team. You can tell Mrs. Stein that she's going to have to find herself another cook and nutritionist."

Mae walked to her desk, sat down, and simply pulled out a checkbook from the top right-hand drawer. "I'll write out your final paychecks," she told Noel.

Rita glared at Noel. "You're not going anywhere," she warned her.

"What?" Noel demanded.

"You heard my sister," Rhonda snapped at Noel. "We're in the middle of an investigation and you're trying to leave. Makes you look guilty, right, Sheriff?"

Brad looked at Noel. "You're not going anywhere until we catch the Street Riders," he said in a stern tone that set Noel back. "As far as we know, you might leave and go warn them that we're setting up this whole sting operation. No, you're staying right here on the property until we say you can leave."

"You can't hold me against my will," Noel hissed. "I know my constitutional rights!"

"Oh please," Rita said in a disgusted voice. "You can't make me believe for a second that you respect the rule of law. You just want to wave the Constitution around when it serves your best interests."

Brad reached behind his back and pulled out a pair of handcuffs, jangling them in the quiet of the nurse's sedate office. "You can either remain here at the property of your own free will or go sit in a jail cell in protective custody until this investigation is through. By the way you're acting, I'm inclined to believe you might be involved with the Street Riders, so maybe we should take you down to the station for some questioning anyway."

"For the last time, I don't know who the Street Riders are!" Noel screeched at the top of her lungs.

"Then why are you trying to leave?" Brad asked. Noel stopped, realizing he had deliberately maneuvered her into a tight corner.

As Brad pushed at Noel's reasoning, Rhonda quickly scanned Mae's face. Mae was staring at Noel with hurt and betrayal in her eyes—eyes that confirmed to Rhonda that the woman was likely innocent of all suspicion that had been tossed in her corner. "I will not stand by and be treated badly by those two," Noel hissed and threw a hard finger at Rita and Rhonda. "This stinks and you know it, Sheriff."

"Oh, pipe down," Rhonda sighed. "You're the one acting like a rotten skunk covered with sewage."

"See?" Noel exclaimed in a screeching tone again. "I'm being harassed."

"Stop playing the victim and grow up," Rita growled. "Just because we stand up to your bullying attitude doesn't mean you're being harassed, got it?" Rita locked eyes with Noel. "You're hereby confined to the first floor of this house. Mae, can we keep them in the kitchen safely?" Mae nodded quickly. "Good. If we catch you outside, or on any other floor, you will be arrested and taken into town. Is that clear?"

"You can't—"

"You heard Detective Knight," Brad warned Noel. "Or do you prefer protective custody?" Noel shut her mouth and an angry shade of red colored her ears and seeped down her neck like a rash.

Mae slowly put the checkbook away with disappointment. She wanted Beth and Noel gone more than anyone, and was not sure why the sheriff didn't throw them into a jail cell right away. Furthermore, she wasn't even sure why the two were trying to quit.

"I know my rights!" Noel hollered, stepping toward Mae with a thunderous look of anger on her face. "You owe us our pay. We're leaving and nobody better stand in our way. Mae, I swear—"

"Put your hands behind your back," Brad ordered Noel and took a step toward her, his hand reaching out to grasp her wrist and pin her against the edge of the desk. "I'm placing you under arrest for obstruction of justice. You have the right to remain silent…"

Noel froze. Fear and panic gripped her mind. Was this hick sheriff within his rights or was he just trying to intimidate her into silence? Only a lawyer would be able to tell her… and she was not a rich woman, so the only way to get in touch with a lawyer was to get arrested, and being arrested was the last thing in the world she wanted. If the sheriff arrested her and tossed her in the can, they would surely go after Beth next, and Beth, that coward, would squeal like a pig and ruin everything.

"Okay…okay!" she said and went limp, putting her other hand in the air in surrender. "I'll stay on the first floor. With Beth. Just don't arrest me. Please, Sheriff."

Brad lowered the handcuffs. "You'll stay in the kitchen."

"The kitchen...okay," Noel agreed, though a rebellious spark gleamed in her eyes like the angry ember glow of a cigarette. "Can I go now?"

"Sure. Just remember…we know how to find you," Rhonda promised with a friendly wink. "Your fingerprints are everywhere."

"That's right. You're in a lot of databases when you work for a retirement home, too," Rita warned Noel. "State licensing boards, insurance companies, payroll, every tax authority you can think of. If you run, we'll flag your bank account, so we'll know where you are if you try to use an ATM, put out a state bulletin for your license plate and license so you can't drive anywhere without getting pulled over. We'll post your picture at every two-bit motel and campground within two hundred miles, so you'll have nowhere to stay. Plus, you can't even buy groceries these days without ending up on security cameras..."

"I hate to give away all our tricks like this, but I just want you to know what you'd be getting into," Rhonda continued with an apologetic smile. "We'll suspend your driver's license. You won't be able to get a job, never mind cash a check. You'll be a fugitive caught in a sophisticated web of surveillance."

"A wanted fugitive with multiple warrants out for her arrest," Rita added. "Probably armed and dangerous, too."

Brad nodded his head. "So you can try and run, and we won't stop you. We'll just let the Feds pick you up later and drag you back here."

Noel could barely believe her ears. Having the full force of justice thrown into her face like a poison pie made her stand in disbelief and shock. "You can't threaten me like this...my lawyer will sue you," she said, trying to sound tough even though her voice shook.

"There are at least three witnesses standing in this room who saw you threaten Nurse Mae," Rita told Noel. "Juries are more inclined to believe an eyewitness account. The more witnesses you get to support the truth, the better, isn't that right, Sheriff?" Brad nodded, slow and regretful, looking at Noel.

Noel slowly backed up against the office door. Outnumbered and furious, her eyes turned murderously angry as she tried to calm herself enough to talk. Her eyes flickered around, looking at each of them in turn. "I'll be down in the kitchen...but you'll regret this," she managed to say, her words weakened by the frightened wobble in her voice. "My lawyer will eat you alive. I'll have your badges before I'm done."

"Let us know when you hear from your lawyer," Rita said with a straight face, knowing full well there was no way Noel could afford one, or that any lawyer would take on such a case.

"Why don't you go downstairs before the sheriff has to escort you and your friend out of this place in handcuffs?" Rhonda added. "Besides, I don't think Mae wants her office to stink like that soup you've been serving any more than it already does." She sniffed pointedly in the direction of Noel's worn green dress.

Noel shot a sour eye at Rhonda as she fumbled to open the door. "You cops stink, you know that? You just think you're above the law and can talk trash to whoever you like, don't you?"

"Nope," Rhonda replied. "People like you stink up the world with your attitude. You're only happy when the whole world is a trash heap. Cops like us just speak plainly about what we see. Now get on back to the kitchen."

Noel snarled at Rhonda and stormed out of the office, slamming the door behind her.

"You were a little rough," Mae said in a worried voice. "If that woman was sent here to kill Lynn Hogan that makes her a very dangerous person in my book. Should we really antagonize her like that?"

"Mae, my sister and I have tangled with some of the worst people this world has to offer," Rhonda said in a calm voice. "We've tangled with murderers, drug dealers, corrupt cops, felons, gangs, and everything else under the sun. You name a type of criminal and we've probably stood in the ring ready to go twelve rounds with him...or her. Noel? She doesn't scare us."

Rita rubbed the tip of her nose and thought for a few seconds. "Mae, do you really believe Kathy Stein sent Noel and Beth here to kill Lynn Hogan?"

"I...deep down? Maybe...yes...I don't know." Mae dropped her eyes. "I can't think of any other reason why she would send two such awful people here. It's too great of a coincidence."

"Then that leaves the question how Rusty Lowly ended up in Lynn Hogan's room holding a knife," Rita said and looked at her sister. "Are you thinking what I'm thinking?"

"The food?" Rhonda asked.

Rita shrugged her shoulders. "It's possible."

"Are you ladies suggesting the food has been tampered with?" Brad asked.

"Yes," Rita said and walked over to the office window and looked out. She gazed at the river sparkling through the trees. For a few seconds, Rita saw herself standing ankle-deep in the river, feeling the cold water whisper past as brightly colored autumn leaves drifted down from the sky. But then reality came flooding back. "He's a stooge," she said.

"What?" Brad asked.

"A fall guy," Rhonda spoke up and leaned back against the office wall. "Mae?" she asked.

"Yes?"

"Can you tell us anything about Lynn Hogan's family?" Rhonda asked. "Sooner or later...possibly sooner...Brad is going to have to contact the family. It would help to have a little information on the people he's going to talk with."

"I'm afraid I don't know very much," Mae confessed. "Lynn Hogan was a resident for a short time. During her stay here I never met any family members. She never made any outside calls, either. Come to think of it, she never even mentioned that she had family."

"What do her records say?" Brad asked.

"Let's see," Mae said and quickly hurried over to the filing cabinet and pulled open the top drawer. "Lynn Hogan..." she said, flipping through a few folders. "Here she is." Mae pulled out a manila folder and opened it. "On the standard intake form, she marked herself as a widow—"

"Wait a minute," Rhonda said, "who brought Lynn Hogan here? We should start with them."

"She showed up in a town car driven by a chauffeur," Mae explained. "No one was with her."

"Okay...what else did she put on her application?" Rhonda asked.

"Prior place of residence was Woodstock, Georgia...occupation she left blank...and...oh, here we are...children..." Mae looked up at Rhonda. "She didn't put down any children."

"You didn't ask for any further details?" Rita asked.

Mae shook her head. "These applications are generic, meant to please the state and nothing else. My job when a person shows interest in becoming a resident here at the home is to reel them in with as much sweet talk as possible." Mae looked embarrassed. "It's something of a sales pitch, I guess. We have ten residents. Each resident pays a pretty penny to live here—"

"How much?" Rhonda asked. "Mae, we need to know."

Mae hesitated and then admitted, "Five thousand dollars a month."

"Five thousand a month...sixty thousand a year…not bad," Rita said, quickly doing the math in her head.

"The money sounds nice," Mae agreed, "except that by the end of each month I barely have enough to cover expenses. The money they pay covers an enormous amount of luxuries." Mae held up her fingers. "Private healthcare...namely me...food, snacks, drinks, free transportation into town, entertainment, arts and crafts, music, outdoor activities like gardening, exercise classes like chair yoga...and much more." Mae lowered her fingers. "Yet the arts and craft room is nearly bare, the pantry is tight, the gas tank of the transportation van is always on empty...I have just enough money left to pay the light bill and squeeze out a few pennies for little repairs and other things." Mae put down the file in her hand. "If it wasn't for those high school kids, this place would be in ruins. When they're not here it takes everything I've got to keep up with the laundry, the cleaning, and other chores. It's not supposed to be like this. When Miss Katherine was alive we had nursing aides to change the beds, full-time groundskeepers, and a house cleaning staff, even a handyman on call...those were the good days."

Rhonda bit down on her lip. "We need to find out if Lynn Hogan has a will and if she has any family members."

Rita looked at Brad. Brad shook his head. "I'm not leaving Rusty. One of you ladies will have to make a trip into town —" before Brad could finish, the phone on Mae's desk rang. Mae closed the filing cabinet and answered the phone.

"Clovedale Falls Retirement Home, this is Nurse Mae," she said.

"Who is it, Mae?" Brad whispered.

"Just one moment, please. It's Billy Northfield," Mae said, putting her hand over the phone. "He's looking for Rita and Rhonda."

Rita looked at her twin and Rhonda shrugged her shoulders. "See what Billy wants."

Rita took the phone from Mae. "Hello, Billy, this is Rita. What's up?"

Billy sighed into the phone. "Well, I sure hate to bother you, but I've got myself a mess on my farm. Heard you were up at the retirement home with Brad, so I thought I'd try to call you."

"What kind of a mess?" Rita asked.

Billy hemmed and hawed for a moment. "Well, you see… seems a knucklehead tourist was caught trying to steal a few bags of apples...some teenager from Boston who figured he'd get his kicks on my dime. Reckon I can't be too hard on him…except the kid punched José right in the nose and pulled a knife on me." Billy stopped and let out another noisy sigh. "Reckon I lost my temper a bit and slapped him blue once I grabbed the knife away. The whole thing didn't sit well with the kid's old man and… well…maybe you can guess what happened next…"

"Oh, Billy," Rita said.

"Yeah, I know," Billy replied. "Me and that kid's old man went a few rounds out back of my apple house...sure made a mess. Bit of trouble, I guess you could say. Reckon the sheriff needs to come on out here." Billy chuckled in embarrassment. "I shoulda stayed at the fairgrounds. I sure was having myself a good time, but I got my farm to tend to and don't have time to stand around gawking at prize pumpkins all day. Shame about the prize, too. I think we grew the biggest pumpkin this year but John O'Neil thinks his will beat mine. John is a good man but he sure likes to let his mouth run braggin' over a whole bunch of nothing, let me tell you—"

"Billy, what about your trouble?" Rita asked.

"Oh," Billy said, "the boy's pa is out cold right now. I mighta...hogtied him and his boy and put them in the back of my truck before they could hurt anyone else. Like I said, bit of a mess. Do you think I should get the sheriff involved or just…kinda…keep it quiet?"

Rita looked at Brad. "Brad, you better take this call."

Brad rubbed the bridge of his nose and then took the call. "Yeah, Billy, what's all this about some trouble?"

"What's wrong?" Rhonda asked Rita.

Rita fought back a grin, grabbed Rhonda's hand, and rushed her out into the hallway, and explained Billy's situation. "Billy said he hogtied the teenager and his dad and put them in the bed of his truck," she giggled. "Poor Billy."

Rhonda laughed. "Billy is something else. I can just see him fighting with a Yankee kid and his dad, falling over baskets of apples, spilling apple cider...my goodness."

Rita giggled again. "Only Billy would knock a man out cold and then hogtie him for good measure," she told Rhonda.

Rhonda put her hand over her mouth to hide her laughter. "What are we going to do with Billy?" she asked.

"I don't know," Rita laughed, forgetting about the murder for a second. But then she spotted Rusty Lowly at the end of the hallway, wandering in confusion, looking around for an escape from his tortured mind. "Oh dear," Rita said and stopped laughing. "We have trouble."

Rhonda turned her head, saw Rusty, and felt her heart break. Yeah, she thought, trouble was in full bloom.

5

Rhonda carefully approached the elderly man who was pacing the hallway muttering to himself in a whisper. "Mr. Lowly?" she asked in a soft, caring voice.

Rusty, as if hearing a distant, strange voice that scared his very soul, startled, looked up at Rhonda and stumbled backward in fear. "Stay away from me!" he cried out.

"Hey...it's okay," Rhonda assured Rusty, keeping her voice soft and caring. "I'm a friend, remember? We met in your room?"

"Stay away from me!" Rusty cried out again and threw his arms over his face. "You want to hurt me...I just know it. No more, no more! It's everywhere…help me…"

Brad came bursting out of Mae's office, saw Rusty stumbling backward, and looked at Rita and Rhonda. "What's going on?"

"Not sure," Rita answered in a worried voice. "We spotted Rusty wandering down this hallway. All we did was say hello."

"Get back!" Rusty begged. "You want to hurt me!"

Nurse Mae brushed past Brad. "Rusty...honey," Mae said in a gentle voice, "it's me, Mae. You're having another episode. Everything is alright."

Rhonda stared at Rusty and waited. Rusty stopped cowering, slowly lowered his arms, and looked at the kind face of the nurse. "Mae?" he asked. Mae nodded her head yes. "Mae, the bad people are back...oh, make them go away," Rusty begged. Rhonda felt her heart break but knew she had to focus. Her eyes locked on Rusty's face and the fear consuming his eyes.

"Rita, I think Rusty has been drugged," Rhonda whispered in an alarmed voice. "Look at his eyes...see how they're dancing back and forth so fast? That's not normal...all his paranoia, confusion...I don't think it's just memory loss."

Rita studied Rusty's eyes and took out a penlight she kept in the pocket of her uniform, quickly checking his pupils. To her horror she found his pupils responded too slowly and unevenly to be the result of anything natural. "Oh my, I think this is a drug reaction," she whispered and quickly looked at Brad. "He's not on any medications that would do this. Get downstairs and arrest Beth and Noel," she pleaded.

Brad stared at Rusty, felt anger grip his chest, and then rushed downstairs. "Mae," Rhonda said in a careful voice,

"Rusty seems to trust you...get him back to his room and keep him there."

"Okay," Mae agreed and cautiously approached Rusty. "Come on, old friend," she said, "let's go take a walk and you can tell me all about the bad people."

"The bad people," Rusty cried in a pathetic, quiet tone, "they're back...and they want to hurt me...they want to steal my memories, Mae. I don't...have many left. It's all slipping away."

"I know, honey," Mae sighed and slowly took Rusty's hand. "Come on, let's get you back to your room."

Rusty stared at Mae, looked into a loving face that brought a little relief to his terrified, confused mind, and reluctantly allowed the woman to walk him back down the hallway.

"Come on," Rita said in a furious voice and stormed downstairs. Rhonda nodded her head and hurried after her sister.

"Hands behind your back...now!" Rita heard Brad yelling as she neared the kitchen doorway.

In the kitchen she saw Brad slapping a pair of handcuffs on Noel. Beth was standing near the back door, scrabbling at the deadbolt on the outside door as if preparing to run. "Don't even think about it!" Rita yelled.

Rhonda quickly yanked her gun out from her ankle holster. "Freeze! Hands in the air," she warned Beth.

"My lawyer is going to eat you alive!" Noel screeched. "You're going to rot in prison for the rest of your miserable lives!"

Beth, clearly understanding that the gig was up and that Noel, the woman she had always depended on for direction, had been reduced to a furious, babbling idiot. Beth raised her hands up into the air. "I...surrender," she said in a cowardly voice. She was face to face with a very hard truth: the hatred in a bully's heart is no protection from the real world. Beth feared, above all, that everything she had ever done with Noel would land her in a very deep pit of trouble.

"Don't say another word, Beth!" Noel hollered.

Brad walked Noel to a wooden chair and sat her down. "You drugged Rusty, didn't you?" he growled. "Before you answer me, you better know a blood test will tell the truth! You want an attempted murder on your record?"

Noel stared up into the sheriff's furious face that reminded her of a fierce German Shepherd. Noel hated dogs...any animal, to be honest; she had never met a dog that had liked her. They were always growling in her direction, snapping at her heels, as if they knew the darkness that lurked inside her. "Talk to my lawyer," she spat at the floor.

Rita erupted in anger. She had had enough of Noel. "Listen," she snapped and yanked out her gun, "we're too far up in the hills for you to be acting the fool like this." Rita walked close to Noel and aimed her gun dangerously near the side of the woman's face, so she could hear Rita's finger settling on the metal of the trigger. "If I fired this gun, no one would hear outside this kitchen except for a few elderly people, half of them too deaf to hear a firecracker, the other half too senile to testify in court. So you better start answering some questions. Is that clear?"

"Are you threatening to kill me?" Noel asked in shock.

Rhonda motioned for Beth to sit down next to Noel. Beth scurried over to sit on the wooden chair next to Noel. "We're not threatening anyone," she said, deciding to break every rule in the book. "We're just stating facts. Isolated up here, isn't it, Sheriff?"

"Yes ma'am, it is."

"Awful important we get some answers before a scuffle breaks out and we have to defend ourselves with our firearms, isn't that right, Sheriff?" Rita added. She fingered the safety on her weapon and looked meaningfully at both women, patiently waiting for them to figure out their next move.

Noel looked at Beth in disbelief. "Maybe...we should talk?" Beth asked Noel. Noel scowled and seemed determined to keep her mouth shut, however.

Rita read Beth's eyes, glanced at Brad, and waited for his approval. Brad nodded his head. "We're up in the mountains," Rita told Noel and Beth. "Poor Rusty needs medical attention so I think we better call the medical evacuation helicopter out from Atlanta."

"Maybe while we're at it, we should call for some state police back-up," Rhonda added, though this was a complete bluff, and she gave Brad a nod so he understood it was simply a ruse.

"Hopefully they get here before that scuffle breaks out with our key witnesses," Rita said. "Just remember…we're not in a city. No maids cluttering up the premises to be witnesses in your corner…no big city lawyers, either. But there's no other staff here to witness what might have happened in the kitchen with poison or whatnot, right? It's the perfect crime, I'd guess. You're out in the stormy sea all by yourself...and whether you make it back to dry land or not..." Rita tapped her gun against her palm, "It's all up to you."

Rhonda grinned. It felt good to give the bad guys a dose of their own medicine. But, Rhonda thought, as the sights, smells, and sounds of the Pumpkin Festival floated back into her mind, it would have felt even better to be at the fairgrounds with her sister, roaming around, eating funnel cakes, drinking apple cider, buying this or that. Instead she was trapped in mud because of two ugly alley cats that were about to learn how painful declawing felt. "We can make you...vanish into thin air. Wonder if anyone would miss you? Maybe...Kathy Stein?"

Beth gulped. She had agreed to work for Kathy Stein in order to earn extra cash to travel around the country with Noel after the job was finished. Now she was in hot water and didn't like the idea of being shipped off to a prison where she would be forced to face the consequences and share her time with women who wouldn't take her lip. The thought terrified her. "I'll—"

"Shut up!" Noel hissed. "Beth, don't say a word...these two...they're bluffing us."

"Are we?" Rita asked. She snatched Noel up by her arm. "Rhonda, take this one out back and do what you will. No one cares and no one will hear, so have at it. I'll deal with the other one."

"Make it quick," Brad ordered in a voice that was so convincing that Beth nearly fainted in shock. "I don't want a mess, either. Got it?"

"Got it, boss," Rhonda said and took Noel by her arm. "Let's go. I don't have all day."

Noel froze. "You can't...I mean...you're cops...I..."

"Shut up and let's go," Rhonda hissed. She pushed Noel toward the back door. "And don't drag your feet."

"Take her out of sight," Brad ordered. "I don't want any mess left behind on the nice lawns."

"I'll shoot her in the river," Rhonda conveyed. "The running water will clear up the blood for me and I'll keep my hands clean." She reached into a box on the counter and took out a pair of sanitary gloves used for food prep. Rhonda snapped them onto her hands quickly and efficiently.

"No!" Noel screamed and desperately backed away from Rhonda. "You can't...I don't want to die." Ugly tears streaked black from her cheap makeup. "Don't shoot me...please."

Seeing that Noel was now broken—which had been very easy to do—Rhonda looked at Rita. "Well?" she asked.

Rita pointed her gun at Beth. "Talk," she ordered.

"Kathy Stein...she hired us," Beth blubbered and looked at her chair. The chair was an island of safety and Noel's terrified but angry eyes across the room reminded her of a shark.

"Can I please sit back down?" Noel begged. Rita motioned toward the chair. Noel ran over and sat back down. "Kathy Stein hired us...I'm not a real nutritionist, okay?"

"And I'm not a medical chef," Beth blurted out. "Mae just gave me a cook book with the special medical diet recipes in it. I've been following it...honest. Our intention wasn't to hurt anyone…except…"

"Who?" Rhonda demanded.

Noel closed her eyes. Surely, she thought, a cold prison cell was waiting for her. "Listen, I was a pharmacist before," she confessed. "I had my license yanked...for looking the other direction when people came in with false or illegal prescriptions."

Brad folded his arms and tossed a 'well done, ladies' nod at Rita and Rhonda. The twin sisters were sure something. "You poisoned Rusty Lowly, didn't you?"

Noel opened her eyes, looked at Beth, and shook her head. "We don't have a choice," she said in a miserable voice and then focused on Brad. "I'll talk if you cut us a deal."

Brad pretended to consider Noel's demand. "No deals. I'll talk with the Feds and see what they can do. That's the best I can offer."

Noel looked at Beth again, panicking. "We better talk...you know Kathy isn't going to save us, she'll just throw us under the bus."

Beth read Noel's eyes and saw that she was truly terrified. "Okay, let's talk."

Noel said, "Kathy Stein hired us to mess with the old man's memory. I swear, we're not connected to that gang thing."

Rhonda pulled up a chair, spun it around, and sat down in front of Beth and Noel. "There is no Street Rider gang," she explained in a laughing voice.

Rita gestured with her gun toward the walk-in freezer. "There is a dead woman in that freezer. We're here to find her killer. Is that clear?"

"A dead woman?" Noel asked in a panicked voice. "Hey, we didn't kill nobody. Kathy only wanted me to mess with that old man."

"We work as a team," Beth explained. "Noel is my sister, like I told you earlier. I didn't need to come along, but Kathy feared that the last chef and nutritionist might not play ball, so she wanted two people who would work as a team."

"Kathy created false credentials for us and sent us up this way," Noel clarified.

Brad wanted to shoot Noel where she sat, but knew prison would be a far worse punishment. "Why did Kathy Stein want Rusty poisoned?" he demanded. Noel and Beth went quiet.

"Talk," Rita snapped and pointed at the walk-in freezer again. "Someone is going to prison for murder."

"We didn't murder anyone," Noel pleaded. "Like I said, Kathy sent me here to mess with that old man—"

"His name is Rusty Lowly," Brad roared. "Stop calling him an old man."

Noel jumped in fear. "Okay, okay...cool down," she begged.

"Kathy wanted Noel to wipe out Rusty's memory," Beth jumped into the fire on scared legs. "Honest, that's all."

"Why?" Brad growled. "Why did Kathy Stein want you to hurt Rusty...steal his entire life?"

Noel lowered her eyes and looked down at the kitchen floor. "Rusty Lowly...there's more to the man than what people know," she said.

"Explain," Brad ordered.

Noel kept her eyes low. "It costs a lot to live here...Rusty Lowly only has a cop's pension. Put two and two together."

"No, you put two and two together," Rita ordered Noel. "Quit trying to weasel out of the truth."

"Rusty Lowly is somehow related to Michael Stonewell," Beth said desperately. "Kathy didn't tell us how and we didn't ask. All she told us is that Rusty is staying here for a few pennies a month. She claims that he's receiving some honorable cop discount or some story like that. I don't know. Kathy didn't talk to me very much."

Rhonda focused on Noel. "I'm sure Kathy talked to you a lot more."

"Sure she did," Noel confessed and dared to raise her eyes. She looked up into a face that understood how to deal with the criminal mind and she looked away again in fear.

"How did you meet Kathy?" Rita demanded.

"I was her pharmacist," Noel confessed. Noel drew in a deep breath and continued on. "Kathy is addicted to pain pills," she explained. "Years back she was in a car accident, hurt her back, and her doctor put her on very strong pain pills. Kathy became addicted...like most people do. When her script ran out and her doctor refused to write another, she began buying on the black market, and that's how we met. No lie."

"There's more," Beth said and nodded at Noel. "Tell them, Noel. Please. I don't want to go to prison."

"And you think I do?" Noel snapped. "Why do you think I'm letting my tongue run loose...you must think I'm stupid."

"No," Beth objected, "I don't think you're stupid. You're very smart...I'm just scared."

"Yeah, join the club," Noel replied. She looked up at Rita again, resigned to their fate. "Kathy likes to gamble...a lot. She owes a lot of bad people a whole lot of money. Between buying her drugs and paying her gambling debts, the woman barely gets by." Noel motioned around the kitchen with her eyes. "This place pays her addiction and gambling debts. Without this place she would be...face down in some alley for sure."

"All Kathy wanted Noel to do was erase Rusty's memory —" Beth began to speak.

"You mean poison an innocent man?" Brad yelled in a disgusted voice. "You were sent here to manipulate his memories...to destroy his entire life! You could have killed him!"

"It was just a...a job to us!" Beth cried out. "We needed the money! Noel's got pharmacist training, she knew enough not to kill him with the medications...probably. Besides, the old man was already losing his memory, weren't we just speeding up the process? What does it matter?"

"It matters to the man who spent a lifetime creating those memories," Brad growled. "Memories of his family...getting married...his childhood...memories of being a cop..." Brad squeezed his hands into two tight fists. "You two are soulless and make me sick."

Rita and Rhonda looked at each other. Rita nodded her head. "Brad, go upstairs and check on Rusty. We'll continue the questioning."

"That's a good idea," Brad agreed, his jaw clenched. "I better leave before I vomit."

Rhonda watched Brad leave the kitchen and then pointed her finger at Noel. "Keep that tongue moving," she said and glanced around the kitchen. "Rita, I want some coffee. See if you can make us a pot, okay?"

"Sure thing." Rita holstered her gun and searched the kitchen for some coffee. It was going to be a long day and she was running on empty.

Noel watched Rita locate the coffee grounds and then begin searching around for a coffee pot. "Kathy is a desperate woman," she said. "She's been able to keep Rusty under lock and key, but she's getting sloppy. A few months ago she got some bad news."

"What?" Rhonda asked. Rita found an old coffee pot on a dusty shelf and blew the dust out of it, coughing as it came up in her face.

"From what Kathy told me, her mother Miss Katherine was always terrified of the Stonewell family, and for good reason. Miss Katherine finally told her daughter, before she died, that Michael Stonewell had descendants and if any of them ever came forward they would be able to take ownership of this mansion by suing the city." Noel watched Rita rinse out the coffee pot and set it down on the kitchen counter. Rita's methodical cleanliness rubbed her the wrong way. The kitchen was starting to feel stuffy if not downright suffocating. "Can we talk outside? I need some fresh air. I won't try to run."

Rhonda glanced at Rita. Rita studied the back door, then hurried to get the coffee brewing. "Okay, outside," she said, turning on the coffee pot. "Beth, you stay right beside your friend or else."

"I will," Beth assured Rita.

Rhonda stood up, walked Beth and Noel out into the crispy afternoon air, and looked around. She spotted a pebble walkway leading into a lovely garden holding a wooden bench under a beautiful flower arbor. "Move," she said and pointed toward the garden. Beth got her legs moving. Noel quickly followed.

"Such a beautiful day," Rita sighed.

Rhonda looked up at a gorgeous tree dropping leaves into the fresh air. They floated down onto her hair. "Are we ever going to be able to enjoy the Pumpkin Festival?" she asked in a sad whisper.

Rita caught a brightly colored leaf with her left hand. "I hope so," she said and walked into the flower garden. "Sit down," she ordered the women.

They sat down on the wooden bench. Noel glanced around. Even though the day was absolutely breathtaking, all she saw was ugliness. Everything was a reminder of how her life had gone sour. Then, out of nowhere, as her eyes watched a leaf dancing in the cool wind, carefree and light, she asked herself a horrible question: "Why is there so much evil stewing inside my heart?" The question terrified her. For the first time in her life, Noel was facing the consequences of the ugliness she had been putting out into the world for years instead of retreating behind the safety of her sharp words. She liked nothing better than to retreat to her favorite websites in her time off, where she could be a beauty queen, surrounded by people who agreed with her, and let off as much bad-mouthed steam as she liked.

Maybe the question burst into her mind because, deep down, Brad's words had finally penetrated her heart. "*You two are soulless and make me sick*," the sheriff had said. Was he right? Had she been stealing a man's entire life away from him, memory by memory? The idea made her ill, and perhaps it truly was worse than murder. *Stop with the guilt...guilt is for the weak*, she reminded herself and forced the monstrous part of herself to retake control and eliminate these soft thoughts that were torturing here. "I have to save my own self...it's each woman for herself now. Forget about Kathy Stein. She'll go down in flames."

"What are you mumbling?" Rhonda asked Noel.

"I said Kathy Stein will go to jail before I do," Noel barked.

"Then you better keep talking," Rhonda ordered.

"Yeah, yeah," Noel replied, feeling brave enough to show a little attitude. As long as she kept her tongue moving, the twin cops surely wouldn't shoot her, and meanwhile she kept thinking and thinking of a way out of this mess. "Kathy swindled some high schools into sending their honor students up to this mansion to work the land and do the house cleaning," she said. "Kathy claimed this place was a historic site or something like, talked to a few people at her country club, and had them start some Preserving Our History school program that received the governor's seal of approval. And money."

"So Kathy Stein knows some influential people," Rita said.

"Kathy's darling husband is some fancy lawyer who mingles with politicians," Noel continued. "The guy is as dumb as he is ugly, to tell the truth. He has no idea that his wife is in trouble with money, and there's no way she is going to tell him. Afraid if she confesses the truth her rich husband might cut her off and toss her out into the wind." Noel made a disgusted face. "She signed a prenup agreement, you see. She doesn't get a penny if he divorces her. Kathy keeps her husband with his nose on the golf course and makes him believe his wife is out planning charity luncheons or garden parties or whatever."

"Surely the husband is involved with the retirement home business," Rhonda said.

Noel shook her head no. "Mr. Fancy Pants is always too busy in court or too busy on the golf course or too busy brown-nosing politicians to even look this way. Kathy said her husband once told her that the 'little house on the hill' she owns is her own play toy and not his. Not like he needs the money anyway. The guy is loaded." Noel looked around. "He wouldn't be happy if he saw Kathy draining their bank accounts."

Rita and Rhonda absorbed Noel's words and began creating a different image of Kathy Stein—not a sweet do-gooder any longer, but a conniving, secretive woman with lots to lose—and the type of social circles she belonged to. "Kathy is hiding her secrets from her husband."

"Yeah, she is," Noel exhaled and nodded. "If Mr. Fancy Pants found out that his wife was pushing nearly a million dollars' worth of debt he'd kick her out into the streets."

Rhonda whistled. "A million dollars."

"Pills cost money...gambling is a way to make money...or lose it. Both are addictive...you figure it out," Noel told Rhonda.

Rhonda was struck by a thought. "Let's go back to the school program."

"That was Kathy's greatest mistake," Noel said. "What started as a clever way to save money turned out to be a curse." Noel looked at Beth. "You tell her."

Beth looked up at Rita and Rhonda. "One of the brats who came here to work decided to stick his nose where it didn't belong."

"We're all ears," Rita told Beth, feeling a sweet taste of autumn wind brush past her mouth. It was s shame to be wasting such a beautiful day on two pieces of mold.

"Kids today know how to dig up anything on the internet," Beth explained. "The kid who came here to work decided to research the complete history of this mansion, from beginning to end...nosy brat."

"Get on with it, Beth," Noel griped.

Beth flinched. "According to Kathy, the kid found out about Michael Stonewell's descendants. How? Who knows…kids today are too smart for their own good."

"To make a long story short," Noel said and rolled her eyes at Beth, "this kid contacted Kathy and started asking questions, wanting to write it up in his school newspaper. He told her what he had found. Kathy hit the roof." Noel struggled against the handcuffs. "Can you take these off?"

"Nope," Rhonda said. "Now keep talking."

Noel mumbled something to herself, insulting the cops in a cowardly whisper they would never hear, and continued. "Whoever this kid was, he was thorough. He created a family tree on Michael Stonewell and planned to interview a few relatives still alive...second or third cousins, people like that. But Rusty Lowly is different."

"How so?" Rita asked.

"Rusty is the son of Michael Stonewell's brother," Noel confessed. "That makes him Michael Stonewell's nephew and closest living relative. I guess Michael Stonewell was considerably older than his younger brother...by twenty years, I think? Somewhere around there...who knows and who cares. All I know about Rusty is what Kathy told me." Noel shook her head. "The high school kid wanted to make his findings public, write a big article, use it in his college applications, but Kathy knew it was too much of a risk. She told me that if he did that, the Stonewell descendants would have grounds to sue the city for ownership of the property and could grab it out right from under her. So she paid the kid off and got him to promise to keep it quiet in the name of 'patient privacy'. You know how high school kids are...she figured out that money overpowers integrity, especially when you get enough to buy a brand new sports car."

"I'm sure Kathy didn't let the matter stop there," Rhonda said.

"How could she?" Noel asked. "She tracked down Rusty Lowly, found him living in some old timers' rest home in Chattanooga...talk about luck." Noel studied the day but still refused to see the beauty breathing before her eyes. "Rusty was in his seventies by then and having a hard time getting by on his own. Kathy knew she had to play it careful...so she brought the guy here."

"To keep close tabs on him, is that it?" Rita asked.

"Rusty has no idea he's related to Michael Stonewell," Noel said with a roll of her eyes. "If Kathy kept him under close watch then she would be able to ensure that the old man would never know the truth. After all, his wife is dead, he has no contact with the other living Stonewell descendents...no one has ever visited him except for that hick sheriff—"

"Watch your mouth," Rhonda warned Noel.

Noel bit down on her lip. "Yeah, Kathy figured it would be...cleaner...to lock Rusty Lowly up in the tower rather than kill him."

"So why did she send you to start poisoning him?" Rita demanded.

Noel stiffened. So did Beth. "Kathy claimed someone contacted her a few months ago, claiming to be a relative of Rusty Lowly, claiming to know the truth about Michael Stonewell and threatening to go public unless Kathy began paying blackmail money."

Rita and Rhonda exchanged glances. "Keep talking."

"Kathy is already up to her ears in trouble," Noel said in a voice that made it plain she found the whole scheme too obvious. "She can't afford to pay out money to some lowlife blackmailer. She's having a hard enough time keeping the state off her back and dealing with her gambling debts. Sure, she could use her husband's influence to push back at the state and give her some relief, but that would mean allowing her husband in on the truth, and that's a big no-no."

"So Kathy figures the best solution is to wipe out a man's memory?" Rita asked.

"No...yes..." Noel struggled. "It's...I just…"

"You what?" Rita demanded.

"I never bought it, but Kathy believes Rusty might know who the blackmailer is, okay?" Noel snapped. "Every morning she had me put a drug into Rusty's food...something with hypnotic effects. At lunch I put a drug in that attacks his memory. We're not just trying to get him to forget..." Noel closed her eyes. "We're trying to find out what he knows."

"When Noel takes Rusty his food," Beth said in a scared voice, "she waits an hour, and then she questions him.

"That was the plan," Noel confessed and slowly opened her eyes. "I really thought I could pull it off but...he's never once come up with a name and I'm not convinced he knows the blackmailer. Besides, the memory loss effect stays in his system far too long and interacts with the hypnotic drug. I've been trying to fix the problem with dosage adjustments...but it takes time, you know, and the old man doesn't always eat every bite..."

Rhonda wanted to slap Noel but held back her hand. "You're altering a man's mind with drugs," she said in a voice that told Noel she was very close to being shot. "You're poisoning him!"

"I...it's just a job," Noel confessed in a sick voice. "He's not dying, okay?" Noel looked at Rhonda. "Kathy didn't want to hurt Rusty, and neither did we. The goal was to get a name and erase a memory...nothing else."

"Then who killed Lynn Hogan?" Rita demanded.

"Not me," Beth blurted out in shock.

"I didn't touch the old woman," Noel insisted. "We didn't even know Lynn was dead."

"What do you know about her?" Rita asked in a tough voice that told Noel she had better speak the truth.

"Nothing," Noel told Rita in a desperate voice. "Kathy never mentioned her to me. My assignment was Rusty Lowly, not some other wrinkly bag of problems—"

"Show some respect," Rhonda snapped, slamming her hand down. "Lynn Hogan is dead."

"So what?" Noel asked. "I didn't know her, did I? Am I supposed to shed tears over some old woman I didn't know? That's not the way the world works."

Rhonda bent down and put her face to Noel's. "In your world, maybe," she growled. "In my world we show respect to the dead. And we show the elderly respect and love. Especially elderly people we work for. Is that clear? You served this woman her food. You served all the residents their food. How can you hate them so much?"

Noel rolled her eyes. "Have you ever been a cook or a waitress? Ever served food, day in and day out, to a bunch of people who don't know your name, probably think you're lower than dirt? I don't work with a bunch of sweet little old elderly people. This isn't some walk in the park. I work with a bunch of sick, bitter, dried-up old husks of humanity."

"Sounds a lot like you," Rhonda told Noel and leaned up. Noel's face twisted in anger but she held her tongue.

"Sure does," Rita agreed. "But this isn't about you. Let's focus back on Lynn Hogan."

"I didn't kill her!" Noel hollered in frustration. "I didn't even know the first thing about her, other than her face and her name. How many times do I have to tell you dimwitted cops that?"

Rhonda looked at Rita. "I hate to admit it, but I think this crocodile is telling us the truth."

"We are," Beth insisted. "Rusty Lowly, he's the man Kathy wanted us to focus on. We don't know nothing about the dead body."

Rhonda bit down on her lower lip. "Think it's possible that the drugs this rat has been putting into Rusty caused him to lose his mind enough that he really did kill her?" she asked Rita with pain in her heart.

Rita did not like the idea. "I'm not sure." Rita focused her eyes on Noel. "We need to know more about the drugs you've been poisoning Rusty Lowly with."

"I'm through talking," Noel informed Rita. "You cops ain't gonna shoot me. You ain't gonna believe me, but you ain't gonna shoot me either. You need me to testify in a court of law. I know how the game works."

Beth looked at Noel with worried eyes. "Don't tempt them," she begged.

"She's right," Rhonda told Beth. "We do need you to testify in a court of law," she explained. "But that doesn't mean we can't find the drugs you've been giving Rusty and feed them to you instead." Rhonda nodded at Rita. "What's good for the goose is good for the gander, right?"

"Right," Rita grinned. "If you refuse to talk," she told Noel, "we'll just have to give you the same treatment you've been giving Rusty."

Noel froze. Her face turned pale. "I...you can't…"

"Can and will," Rita promised Noel. "So you can either keep talking or we can start experimenting on you."

"I like experiments," Rhonda said in a dangerous voice. "I liked dissecting frogs in school." Rhonda locked her eyes on Noel. "You look like a good frog to dissect. Lots of nice juicy brain bits to pick apart."

"You're...insane," Noel whispered.

"We'll see," Rhonda promised Noel. "Rita, go find the drugs."

"No, wait...I'll talk, I'll talk," Noel cried out in fear. "Just...don't put that poison in me. I'm a human being for crying out loud."

Rhonda grabbed Noel's chin. "And so is Rusty Lowly, you piece of trash," she hissed. "Your time of hurting people has come to an end. It's time to face the truth and the consequences, which is going to be the rest of your life behind prison bars." Rhonda let go of Noel's chin and studied the scenery, heaving a deep breath to calm herself and focus on the task at hand. Sure, she had two monsters in custody but from the sound of things, there remained another monster still crawling around in the dark.

6

Brad refused to go back to town. "You ladies go handle Billy's problem," he said taking a sip of coffee. "I'll keep watch here."

Rita glanced at Beth and Noel. Noel had her left wrist handcuffed to Beth's right wrist. "Brad, we also need to get these two behind bars and run Rusty's blood to the hospital for testing. And what about looking up Ollie and Patty in the database? We don't have time to—"

"I'm not leaving Rusty," Brad said in a voice that told Rita she was fighting a losing battle. "You ladies stick those two in a jail cell, run Rusty's blood to the hospital, and then go check on Billy. The rest can wait. I'm staying right here with Rusty and that's final."

Mae poured herself a cup of coffee. "I've contacted the hospital," she explained with a sigh. "Dr. Downing has been notified and is waiting for the blood I drew from

Rusty. We don't have time to stand here and bicker with one another."

"Brad, we still don't know who killed Lynn Hogan," Rhonda pointed out. "What if the killer is still stalking these halls?"

"I'm sure Rusty killed Lynn," Mae told Rhonda in a miserable voice. She threw an angry glare at Noel. "Now that we know the truth...what other explanation is there?"

Rita watched Mae sip at her coffee. The poor woman looked miserable and in no mood to be argued with. "Mae, according to those two someone is blackmailing Kathy Stein. The killer could be the blackmailer...or Kathy Stein herself. It's not safe—"

"I'm no greenhorn," Brad told Rita in a stern voice. "I've taken down my share of killers. If the killer shows up I'll handle him...or her. You ladies just do as I tell you. I'm still the sheriff in this town."

"But—" Rhonda tried to object.

"Go," Brad ordered and pointed at the kitchen door. "I don't have time to argue. And..." Brad lowered his eyes, "I'm inclined to agree with Mae...Rusty probably killed her, believing she was one of those mean people he keeps claiming are trying to hurt him." Brad sighed. "At least no jury will condemn him for acting out of defense, and...I guess Rusty will spend the rest of his days here."

"Then why haven't you contacted backup or forensics, Brad?" Rhonda asked. "If you really believe Rusty killed Lynn, why are you still hiding her body in that freezer?"

Brad raised his eyes. "A good cop never puts all of his apples in one barrel," Brad answered. "Until I know for certain I'm not making a single call to the suits. Now," he said and pointed at the kitchen doorway again, "get moving."

"Come on, Rhonda," Rita said, "there's no sense in standing here wasting time. The sooner we get to town and get back the better."

Rhonda took out her gun. "Move," she told Beth and Noel.

"Here," Brad said and tossed Rita the keys to his patrol car. "Don't speed. Take the curves slow and watch out for deep cuts in the road going down."

Rita caught the car keys. "We will," she promised and walked out of the back door, turned around, and waited for Beth and Noel to appear. "Nice and slow," she ordered. "No tricks."

"Where do you think we would go?" Noel hissed. She raised her left wrist up in the air, dragging her sister's handcuffed wrist along. "We can't exactly run a marathon."

Rhonda closed the back door. "Enough with the lip," she snapped. "Get moving."

"Yeah, yeah," Noel groused. She followed Rita around the mansion, passing beautiful flower gardens lightly blanketed with autumn leaves. They made their way to Brad's car, Noel practically dragging Beth along with her.

"Your limo," Rita said and snatched open the back door. "In."

Noel shot Rita a snotty look and crawled into the back seat. Beth hurried awkwardly after Noel.

Rhonda slammed the backdoor shut. "I can drive," she told Rita, with a depressed sigh. "Rita, we have to find out if Lynn has a will." Rhonda glanced up to the front of the retirement home and shook her head. "This place is so beautiful. Why, I could just melt standing here. And listen to the river...so peaceful."

"I know what you mean," Rita replied. "Murder sure has a way of turning beauty into mud, doesn't it?"

Rhonda nodded her head. "All I want to do right now is go walk along the river...listen to the wind...watch the leaves fall and rest. Instead my mind is racing with questions and my heart is full of anxiety." Rhonda glanced around. "Rusty didn't kill her, Rita."

"Surely not," Rita whispered. "And he definitely isn't the blackmailer. Someone is around here someplace. Possibly the killer."

Rhonda kept her eyes moving. "We need to make contact with Kathy Stein," she pointed out. "Kathy didn't answer her cell phone when we had Noel call her. My guess is she's either hiding or she's on this property watching every move we're making."

"It's also possible the blackmailer might have grabbed Kathy," Rita noted.

Rhonda nodded her head. "Yep."

Rita studied the landscape and then focused on the mansion. "No sense in wasting time," she said and hurried around to the driver's side door, pulled it open, and jumped. Rhonda climbed into the passenger seat and buckled up.

"We should talk about what to do first—" Rita began to speak as they began moving the car back down the mountain, but stopped when her cell phone began to ring. Rita reached into her purse and snatched it out. "It's Billy."

"You better answer it," Rhonda said. Rita hit the speakerphone button while easing the car toward the front gate. A sensor attached to the gate detected the car and the gates slowly opened.

Rita checked on Beth and Noel in the rearview mirror, spotted them looking down at their hands instead of enjoying the surrounding beauty, and then said. "Hey, Billy."

"Got some good news for you," Billy said in his most charming southern drawl. Rita could just picture him leaning against the tailgate of his truck, staring out at a wide pumpkin patch filled with bright orange pumpkins. In the background she could hear happy visitors and tourists searching the field for the perfect pumpkin to pick and buy.

"I could use some good news," Rita told Billy as they eased through the gate.

"I let that fella from Boston and his son go," Billy said in an easy voice. "The fella came to his senses, gave me a proper apology, and offered to leave town if I promised not to let the sheriff loose on him. Reckon that seemed fair enough. I ain't interested in having the law out here with all of these tourists wandering about. Hoping you can pass the word along to Brad for me about that…" Billy paused and she could hear the low whine of a hound dog in the background. "Oh, boy," Billy said in a worried voice, "come here, boy! Good boy. Here's Chester, Mr. Droopy himself, coming to let me know I forgot to fill his food dish. Whenever he walks with his head down it's always bad news."

Rita felt a grin touch her face. "Well, sounds like you have had a busy morning," she pointed out, hearing the sound of people talking and children laughing in the background. "Billy, where are you right now?"

"Why, I'm right near the pumpkin patches," Billy explained and ruffled Chester's long ears. "I got pumpkin patch duty this afternoon. Somebody's got to watch these folks and help 'em when they get stuck in the mud or can't figure out how to get a pumpkin off a dang vine." Chester kept flapping one ear. "Maybe I got into a bit of a wrestling match earlier...had to set a big city Yankee fella and his boy straight...now listen, Chester, stop with the ear...I know you're hungry..."

Rita grinned again. "Chester is really letting you have it, isn't he?"

"Boy, I'll say he is...grumpy dog," Billy complained. He whistled over to his farmhand. "José, when you get a minute, run up to the house and feed Chester." José hollered over for Chester and the old dog slowly turned to plod back toward the main farmhouse. "You're welcome! Ungrateful ol' hound…" Billy hollered after Chester. "Well, there he goes," Billy told Rita and let out a sigh of relief. "That dog can be mighty fussy at times."

"I bet," Rita agreed. "I'd rather have a day with your fussy hound dog than the day I've had…" She wished she was at Billy's farm, wandering through the pumpkin fields, drinking apple cider, and basking in the beautiful day. "But enough about that. I'm glad you settled your problem peacefully. Brad sent us out to do a few things and we were going to stop by…I guess you don't need us to come to your farm anymore."

Billy made a noncommittal sound. "Well, that ain't exactly so," he said. "I was kinda hoping you girls might drop by for a visit, seeing how the trouble is over. That is, if you ain't busy, I mean?" Billy cleared his throat nervously and suddenly sounded a touch more formal than usual. "If you please, I mean...I thought it might be mighty nice since Brad is sending you girls into town..."

Rita smiled. Billy was so sweet. "Well Billy, I sure appreciate it. Rhonda and I have to take two criminals and drop them off at the jail. Then we have to drive to the hospital and see Dr. Downing. I wish we had time to visit you today but—"

"Oh…no, no," Billy said in a quick, nervous voice, "I understand. If there's one thing Billy Northfield understands it's that you gals get mighty busy working cases for the sheriff. Yes sir...ma'am...and when folks get busy chores wait for no man. My daddy always said a man who ignores his chores won't have no food come winter, and no one to even keep him warm while he starves. That's what my daddy always said."

Rita could have reached through the phone and hugged Billy. "Rhonda and I will come out for a visit as soon as we can. We promise."

"We promise," Rhonda said in a voice loud enough for Billy to hear.

Billy made an embarrassed but pleased sound. "I reckon...I better get out to the pumpkins," he said and cleared his throat again. "I'll see you soon. It'll be a delight, ma'am. Bye."

"Bye, Billy." Rita ended the call and sighed. "Billy is such a sweet man."

Rhonda glanced at her sister. "Hey, I know that look." Rita grinned and eased the car over a deep rut in the road.

"What look?" Rita asked and stiffened up. "There's no look, Rhonda. You...focus on all we have to do!"

"Sure there isn't," Rhonda teased Rita.

Rita rolled down the window for some air, suddenly feeling a little bit hot. She huffed. "You're impossible, Rhonda Knight."

"What are you, a third grader?" Rhonda continued to tease her sister. "We're grown women. We should be able to discuss matters..." Rhonda paused for effect and then raised her eyebrows and said: "Practically."

Rita threw a hard look at Rhonda. "Don't start," she warned.

Rita eased around another sharp curve. "All I'm saying is that Billy is a really nice guy. You could do a whole lot worse."

"I do not have any romantic inclinations toward Billy Northfield. Why, I barely know the man," Rita fumed, her cheeks turning pink. "You're the one who has a schoolgirl crush on him."

"I sure do," Rhonda smiled fondly, "but not in the way you think. Billy is a sweet man, one of the best in my book, but I like him as a friend. Or a brother, perhaps. Sooner or later his personality and mine…we would grind each other into the dirt." Rhonda glanced at her sister. "Billy needs a woman with a more practical attitude toward life...no offense."

Rita looked at Rhonda. "None taken. But what do you mean?" she asked.

"Well," Rhonda explained, "Billy is a down-to-earth man. He's a farmer, for goodness sake! He lives a simple life.

He knows his cows, his apple orchards, his pumpkin patches. He can hogtie a person in seconds. But," Rhonda continued, "what Billy doesn't have is a sensible woman to...educate him about the finer points of...well, things he doesn't know."

"Such as?" Rita asked. Noel and Beth were still silent in the backseat, and could not hear them very well through the divider in the sheriff's car. Rita looked out at the passing wooded slopes of the hills and sighed. "Maybe I need to be educated, too."

"Rita," Rhonda said in exasperation, "I'm not saying I'm some kind of expert. You know me...I read comic books on the toilet. I mean, I can tell you more about Archie and Jughead—at least in the older comics—than I can tell you about how to make a roast beef for Sunday supper or how to properly iron a shirt. I wear fuzzy pink bunny slippers, eat sugary cereal at midnight—even though I know better—and still bathe with my first rubber ducky. I watch reruns of Tom and Jerry and the Andy Griffith Show, and listen to music from old Looney Toons cartoons when I go jogging."

"You're messed up," Noel said in a loud mutter through the seat divider.

"Hush up," Rhonda ordered Noel, "this conversation doesn't involve you."

Rita focused, thinking. "I read more about John Quincy Adams than Archie Andrews. I always make the Sunday roast and have been collecting recipes in my little tin since

I was a teenager. I wear sensible slippers while I knit. I do all our ironing because you always mess up the cuffs and collars. I never eat at midnight and certainly never that ghastly children's cereal…and no rubber duckies for me. I watch documentaries and cooking shows and listen to motivational talks when I go running…while the bran muffins are baking for breakfast."

"Exactly," Rhonda nodded her head. "We're opposites in so many ways…you're the kind of woman who would feed Billy's chickens at dawn every day and make sure he wore a warm scarf in cold weather, and have dinner ready at exactly the right time—"

"Well, that's easy, Billy eats supper at five o'clock because that's when the cows are in the milking barn…" Rita said automatically and blushed, realizing how much she already knew about him.

"See? That's what Billy needs. A woman's touch – practical but thoughtful in all the right ways. In some ways he's a lot like me…"

"You're nothing like him," Rita pointed out with a laugh. "It would take a whole platoon of psychiatrists to figure you out."

Rhonda smiled. "I'll take that as a compliment," she said. "My point is that opposites do attract, and for good reason, but a circus clown like me could never manage the serious, practical life of a farmer's wife. Billy tolerates my silliness…but he admires you. He might even adore you. My point is that he needs someone like you."

"Look," Rita said, putting an end to the conversation, "Billy is a nice guy, and yes, I like him...but as a friend. I've never even gone on a date with the man, and here we are drawing up my future life with him? No. Besides, I could never see myself falling in love with a man like Billy, as sweet as he is. I'm sure someday the right man will come along. But for now let's focus. We're on a case and we need to focus on catching a killer."

Rhonda shrugged. "If you say so," she said. When the wheels of the car finally hit pavement Rhonda sighed in relief.

"Besides," Rita added quietly, "if I ran off and got married to some farmer, who would bake the bran muffins for my dear sister?"

Rhonda patted her sister's hand and smiled. "Don't you worry. I'll buy my fruity sugar cereal in bulk and visit you every Sunday for your roasts. Deal?"

"Deal."

"We need to make good time," Rita said as she turned onto the main road, "so hold on because I'm going to break the speed limit." She hit the gas and they sped toward town.

Far up the hill, Clovedale Falls Retirement Home appeared silent in the sunny day. Then a strange figure slithered out from behind a tree, hurried to a locked basement door, pulled out a key, and glanced around. "All clear," the figure whispered, then unlocked the basement door and vanished inside. "Sheriff Bluestone, you're next on my list.

You should have left when you had the chance. Now you must die...you all must die."

Brad stood in the kitchen drinking coffee with Mae, still musing over the events of the day and trying to figure out what to do. The clock was ticking and with each passing second his hands were becoming more and more tied and he did not know how much longer he could delay calling the coroner. "Rusty...be innocent," he whispered in a weak voice, waiting for the Knight sisters to call him with some news. "Please be innocent," he whispered in prayer.

Rusty didn't hear Brad. He was up in his room staring into the past at a strange memory.

Noel and Beth cringed back against each other when Rita slammed the cruel, cold cell door shut. "Make yourselves comfortable," Rita said, "because you're going to be here a while."

"I want to call my lawyer," Noel insisted.

Beth looked at the hard, bumpy-looking cot, felt panic grab her heart, and grabbed the bars of the cell door. "Please, let me out!" she begged. "This is...I'm not a criminal. I'm—"

"Give it a rest, sister," Rhonda told Beth. "You helped your sister damage the memory of an innocent man. And now you're exactly where you belong."

"But...but..." Beth tried to object. And then it struck her:

justice had captured her crooked heart and thrown it into a deep pit.

"Save it for the judge," Rita said. She looked at Noel with a hard eye. "You'll get your call, whenever someone gets around to you."

Noel, feeling somewhat safe behind bars, decided to throw a temper tantrum. "You think you're something, don't you?" she hissed. "You're nothing...a nobody! Do you hear me? This country belongs to people like me, people who are going to change the culture and get rid of cops like you—"

"And turn the culture into what? Into a trash heap filled with rats like you?" Rhonda finished and tapped the cell bars with her nails. "You're exactly where you should be."

"That's right," Rita nodded her head. "Where's your precious culture change now? Your hippie ideals? We're not the ones locked up behind bars. We're not the ones out there poisoning innocent old men just to earn a buck. We're the ones putting people like you behind bars. And someday, when you're old, bitter, and alone—after you get out of prison for murder, of course—you'll think back to this day and know that your kind lost. Why? Because justice is on our side, not yours. Justice will always live in the hearts of those who stand for truth." And with those words Rita made her way back outside, leaving Noel fuming and Beth terrified.

"Off to the hospital," Rhonda said, walking out into a soft wind full of falling leaves. She took a second to soak in the sight of the leaves raining down from brightly colored trees, the wind-blown leaves whisking up and down the sidewalk lined with pumpkins and haybales outside of the cozy shops and storefronts. Clovedale Falls wasn't known for crime so the police station with its three tiny jail cells was right next to a few adorable stores—a hardware store, a feed store, a dress shop—none of whom worried about being next door to criminals. "Smell that wind."

Rita looked up and down the sidewalk, spotted a few kids riding their bikes, two old ladies looking into the display window of the dress shop, an old man entering the hardware store, and smiled. "This is what life is supposed to be like," she said in a peaceful voice as a leaf landed in her hair. She gently retrieved it, kissed it, and tossed it back into the wind. "Fly free, sweet baby."

"Are you becoming a poet?" Rhonda smiled.

"Maybe," Rita smiled back and watched the two old women finally enter the dress shop. "People are poetry in a way...their hearts either sing with beauty or scribble ugliness." Rita pointed at the group of kids riding their bikes. "Look at those kids...free as a song."

"It's been a while since I've seen kids out riding their bikes," Rhonda nodded. "It's a beautiful sight. And just listen to them...teasing each other..." Rhonda watched one of the kids try to ride without hands and then nearly crash into a mailbox. "Oh my," she laughed and then called out: "Be careful." The kid, embarrassed by his clumsy riding, waved a hand at Rhonda and the raced off down a leaf soaked street and vanished into a residential neighborhood lined with cozy cottages. His friends gave pursuit and soon vanished out of sight as well. "Kids," Rhonda laughed again.

Rita leaned against the driver's door of Brad's car and sighed. "Rhonda, we moved to Clovedale Falls to get away from crime. And now look at us...right back in the frying pan."

"I know," Rhonda said and leaned back next to her sister. "We should be at the Pumpkin Festival having the time of our lives." Rhonda looked at Rita. "Wish I could come up with a joke right about now, but I can't."

Rita sighed. Rhonda sighed. They stood in silence for a few minutes. "Guess we better get to the hospital so we can get the results up to Brad."

"Guess so," Rhonda agreed, and began to open the driver's side door when a voice called out.

"Ladies...uh, ladies..." A man called out, running down the sidewalk toward them.

"Huh?" Rhonda turned her head and spotted the tall, lanky figure of local reporter Mark Bricker loping in their direction. "Oh no, it's Mark," she whispered to Rita.

Rita spotted Mark, wondered if they could make a run for it, and then decided it was too late. "Boy, is this luck or what," Mark said running up to Rhonda and Rita with a big friendly grin. "I've been looking all over for you two."

"Why would that be?" Rhonda asked Mark with her best patient smile.

Mark brushed a leaf off his white button-up oxford and then wiped his hands nervously over his tan khaki pants. He was forty-one and known around town as a bit of a nerd, built tall and narrow like a wiry scarecrow with a few gray hairs in his mop of black curls. He was single, still lived with his mother, and drove a car almost as old as he was, but he was a brilliant, dogged reporter, despite his nervous demeanor.

Mark smiled nervously. He quickly tossed a thumb at Brad's car. "I saw you two leave the fairgrounds this morning with the sheriff," he said. "What's going on?" Mark pulled a narrow reporter's notepad out of his pocket and poised his pencil to take notes.

"Nothing is going on," Rhonda told Mark and eased the driver's side door open. "The sheriff just needed a little extra...help, that's all."

"Help doing what?" Mark persisted. "Investigation? Evidence gathering? Why are you driving his car without him?"

"Uh...he just sent us on an errand," Rita quickly came to the aid of her sister. "Now, if you will excuse us."

Mark deliberately sat down on the hood of Brad's car and began rubbing his back as he continued to catch his breath. "Can you ladies give me a minute," he begged. "My old football injury...running down the sidewalk like that...I need a rest."

Rhonda rolled her eyes. "You told us you never played football, Mark."

"Off the hood," Rita ordered.

Mark shook his head. "Look, ladies, I'm going to get the details sooner or later," he confessed. "You might as well give me the correct details so I can get the word out, right? Besides, there's only so much a man can write about pumpkins and hayrides. I need a real story, like the investigation you ladies brought to town when you arrived. That was some story."

"We didn't bring a story to town, Mark," Rhonda insisted. "We just—"

"A murder...a twisted plot...the Mafia...a beautiful villain...that's stuff right out of the movies," Mark told Rhonda in an excited voice. "Those are the kind of stories I'm after. If I write about one more prize pumpkin I'm going to pull my hair out." Mark remained on the hood and crossed one ankle over the opposite knee. "I've spent my entire life here in Clovedale Falls, you know," he explained. "I reckon I'll die and be buried here, too. And I'm okay with that because I sure do love this little town. But sometimes a man needs some danger...some excitement...some bullets flying in the air. Real stuff...real journalism."

Rhonda understood Mark's frustration. Mark was a decent guy whose nerdy demeanor hid a creative streak and a need for excitement; and, she thought, gazing idly at him in the golden sunshine maybe his nerdy demeanor hid a handsomeness she had never noticed before either. When he got excited about something, his curls flopped down a little bit on his forehead and he looked like a young Marlon Brando but without the brooding. Mark was a six foot tall ray of sunshine.

All Mark wanted was a good story to bring some life to his beloved newspaper. Was it a crime to feed him a few details? Yet Rhonda hesitated. "Mark, I wish we could help you, but my sister and I are really busy."

"Doing what?" Mark asked in a hopeful voice. "And don't say helping the sheriff with personal stuff. I know Brad and the only personal stuff he has going on is picking up enough bait for fishing on his day off."

Rita looked at Rhonda and shrugged her shoulders. Like Rhonda, she thought Mark had a decent brand of humanity in his heart; however, a murderer was on the loose and there was no time to talk to the local press (especially when the press was a one-man show and that one-man show seemed to make her sister's eyes light up lately). "Mark, I'll give you a lead...talk to Billy. Yeah, that's a good idea. Billy got into a fight with a man from Boston and had to hogtie him."

Mark rolled his eyes. "Billy has hogtied lots of folks. Last year he hogtied two guys from California who insulted old Chester. Billy gave them a real whooping, hogtied them, and then threw them in the bed of his truck."

Rita giggled. "Really? Is this a habit of his? He didn't mention that on the phone."

Mark nodded. "Not a year goes by that Billy doesn't tangle with a tourist or two and hogtie them." Mark looked around the small town he loved. "Most tourists are nice folks, but you get some rotten tomatoes with attitudes that pass through. Billy is a nice guy, one of the best in my books, but he don't take lip from tourists." Mark grinned. "When Billy was younger he tangled with a few bikers who rolled into town. Boy, did Billy take a whooping, but he sure gave a whooping back. And do you know, until this very day those same bikers come our way just to say hello to Billy?"

"Really?" Rita asked, pleased.

"Billy takes them to his church picnic, in fact," Mark explained. "He turned a group of dangerous bikers into some pretty good fellas who visit once a year and take their ministry on the road." Mark smiled. "I wrote a whole feature about it. Their ministry helps bikers leave the gang life and turn to the Lord. Amazing how a well-timed incident can change your life, isn't it? Only Billy would end up making friends that way."

"That sounds like Billy," Rita said with a soft smile. Rhonda looked at her with a smirk. "What?"

"What my foot," Rhonda smirked.

"Don't start," Rita sighed. "Mark, we have to go."

"Okay, okay," Mark said, giving in. "I guess I'll wander back to the fairgrounds and see if there's been any trouble. Maybe somebody stole a funnel cake or a bale of hay," he chuckled. "Or hey, maybe somebody didn't pay for a pony ride. Or better yet, maybe somebody is lost in the corn maze. Oh, I better hurry!" He rolled his eyes good-naturedly and winked at the twin sisters.

Rhonda reached out and patted Mark on the arm. "You're blessed to live in this town and own a newspaper, Mark. Don't throw your blessings down onto the ground."

Mark looked into Rhonda's beautiful eyes and almost had to stop himself from declaring his love for her in that instant. Instead he sighed and scratched the back of his head bashfully. "I know I'm blessed, and I actually love the Pumpkin Festival so much I don't care if I have to write a week of silly stories," he confessed. "A man craves a juicier story sometimes, that's all." Mark tossed his thumb at the jail. "Nothing in there except cobwebs. Now, don't get me wrong, that's a good thing for a town, but not for a newspaper. I'll see you ladies later, I hope." Mark looked at Rhonda again, offered her a bright but shy smile, and wandered down the street.

"Poor guy," Rhonda told Rita. "I guess I can't blame him for wanting a story."

Rita watched Mark walk down the sidewalk scattered with leaves until he disappeared around a corner. "He's so nerdy," she complained. "He reminds me of our high school math teacher. That red bow tie!"

"Oh, it's cute, leave him alone."

"I'm not insulting the guy," Rita insisted. "I feel sorry for him. Somebody needs to teach him some confidence and how to comb his hair...and for crying out loud, a man his age shouldn't be living at home." Rita shook her head. "You're telling me all about Billy Northfield, well Mark Bricker needs a good woman, too."

"Yeah, a good woman," Rhonda sighed, staring at the corner where Mark had disappeared. She looked at Rita. "We better get to the hospital."

Rita nodded and climbed into the front passenger seat. "Back to work," she said and buckled up.

Rhonda eased Brad's car out onto the front street. "Brad once told me Mark was engaged to be married a long time ago," she told Rita, feigning nonchalance.

"He did?" Rita asked and rolled down the passenger side window. "Air feels so nice."

"It sure does," Rhonda agreed, stopped at a four-way stop, hung a right, and aimed the car toward the hospital. "From what Brad told me, Mark was engaged to his high school sweetheart."

"Oh, that's sweet," Rita said, watching the cozy neighborhood with its streets lined with warm ranch style houses and cottages, drenched with bright autumn leaves, front porches decorated with pumpkins and hay bales leading into warm kitchens no doubt filled with the smell of pumpkin pies.

"It would have been sweet," Rhonda continued, spotting a bunch of bikes in a heap in a front yard belonging to one of the cottages. "Guess the kids decided it was time for a snack," she said.

"Guess so."

Rhonda drove past the bikes and then let her mind return to Mark. "Mark's high school sweetheart decided Clovedale Falls wasn't her cup of tea anymore and ran off with some soldier boy stationed at Fort Stewart. Mark has never seen her since...according to Brad, that is."

"That's sad, Rhonda, but a man moves on with his life," Rita pointed out. "A broken heart heals with time."

"I know that," Rhonda replied. "People heal in different ways. Mark honestly thought he was going to marry his high school girlfriend and now what? He looks like the same lost, nervous high school kid who had his heart broken all those years ago. Mark's faith in love must have been crushed."

Rita looked at her sister. "Now who is getting stars in her eyes?" she teased.

"Ha, ha, very funny," Rhonda groaned. "All I'm saying is that we can't judge Mark because he's over forty and still living at home with his mother. I mean, Mark does own a newspaper—"

"A newspaper he inherited from his daddy," Rita pointed out.

Rhonda sighed. "Okay, okay, so Mark caught a break, is it a crime to live with your parents before marriage?" she asked.

"Aw, Rhonda, you're defending him."

"I'm not defending him," Rhonda insisted in a weak voice. "All I'm saying is that there's no reason to kick dirt in his face. I mean, let's face it, Rita, Mark is a gem. I would rather date a man living happily at home with his mother than some guy living in a bachelor pad who brings a different girl home every Friday night."

Rita laughed. "Bachelor pads? The seventies are over, Rhonda. It's hardly disco balls anymore. It's normal for singles to live on their own."

"Maybe, but so many single men still think buying a gal dinner should be their entrance ticket to the circus. Old fashioned romance…an old-fashioned man with good manners…is hard to find." Rhonda turned onto Pumpkin Seed Street, then pulled to a stop beside a warm two-story blue house. "Is it so bad for a woman to want a home full of children...and a loving husband?" she asked.

Rita looked at the two-story house, spotted a woman raking leaves, and sighed. "I think we both want to grow old...with someone to love by our side," she said and patted Rhonda's arm. "We just have to be patient. We're not asking too much out of life. Listen, we have to get moving, okay? We have work to do. We can talk about Mark later." Rhonda nodded her head and drove away. The woman raking leaves looked up, spotted the car driving away, and then looked around the sweet autumn day. A darkness was in the air, she thought, shivering all over as she returned to raking the endless piles of leaves.

7

Rita waited in the car while Rhonda ran Rusty's blood work into a one-story brick building that had been built in 1958, according to the bronze plaque mounted proudly by the main entrance. The building housed the Clovedale Falls Hospital, which to Rita and Rhonda's disappointment was nothing more than a glorified first aid station. But beggars can't be choosers. Rita felt confident that the hospital could handle a broken leg and call in a medical evacuation helicopter for anything serious; or at least, so she hoped.

"Still," Rita mused, studying the aging brick building with curious eyes, "it sure is quaint. Nice mums blooming in the flower beds...trimmed lawns...more like a school than a hospital."

As Rita idled in the car, Billy pulled into the emergency parking lot, admonished Chester to mind his manners, and made his way out. As he did, his eyes roamed over the small visitor parking lot and spotted Brad's car. "Well, I'll be," Billy said, seeing Rita sitting in the car pretty as a picture. Just as he had hoped. He scratched his neck for a moment, then dusted off his overalls, settled his hat more firmly on his head, and walked over to her.

Rita spotted Billy's familiar form walking toward her and a big smile broke out on her face. She hurried out of the car.

"Well, howdy," Billy waved. "Fancy meeting you here."

"Hello," Rita waved back as a strong gust of wind caught her hair, scattering her skirt around her for a moment so she was forced to smooth it back down with an embarrassed but cute grin. "My, the wind is picking up."

Billy watched the wind play softly in Rita's hair. He had never seen anything more beautiful in his life. "Thought I might, uh…find you here," he asked.

Rita pointed at the hospital. "Rhonda is inside."

"Nothin' happened to her, has it?" Billy asked in an alarmed voice.

"No, no, she's just dropping off...uh, something Dr. Downing needs," Rita explained. "What about you, Billy? Are you okay?"

"Oh sure," Billy said and threw his right hand at the wind. "Billy Northfield is tougher than nails. I'm here because one of my workers twisted his ankle in a pretty bad way. Came to check on him and give him a ride back home and I remembered you said on the phone you might be stopping by here…" Billy spotted a bench a short distance away under a tall pine tree. "Uh, got a minute to sit?"

"I do," Rita smiled. "But I shouldn't keep you…"

"Nah," Billy explained. "Juan is having his ankle tended to. My backside will grow sore sitting in that waiting room before he's ready to go home." Billy looked at the emergency entrance. "Juan is the clumsiest fella on earth, but I sure like him. He's a good daddy and a good husband, too. Man can't ask for nothing more. Reckon it ain't his fault he's so clumsy."

Rita saw a tenderness in Billy's eyes that warmed her heart. "Let's sit down."

Billy smiled, walked Rita to the bench, and nervously sat down beside her. "Uh...mighty nice day, huh?"

"Beautiful," Rita agreed, watching leaves swirling gently from the trees across the street. She looked at Billy and tried to suppress the butterflies that persisted in fluttering in her stomach. "How's everything on your farm?"

"Why, I'm almost sold out of pumpkins and the festival ain't even half over," Billy said in a proud voice. "I'm going to have to open my north field up. I never open up my north field until the festival is almost over." Billy glanced around and then whispered in a secretive voice. "My east field grows the best pumpkins. My north field ain't so good...I sell those pumpkins at a lower price, but don't tell nobody."

"Your secret is safe with me," Rita giggled.

The sound of a giggly Rita placed a sweet peace in Billy's heart and an awed smile on his face. He watched Rita with curious eyes, a smile crinkling the corners and then glanced in the direction of his truck. The last thing he wanted was for Rita to ask him not to stare at her. He cleared his throat nervously. "Chester gets cranky when he has to come to the hospital with me."

Rita found Billy's truck, spotted Chester in the passenger seat with his tongue lolling out, and giggled again. "Chester seems cranky pretty often."

"I'm telling you," Billy exclaimed. "Don't matter how busy I am, when he gets hungry he makes it known to the world." Billy shook his head. "Sometimes I wonder why I put up with that dog."

"You love him," Rita told Billy simply.

Billy lowered his chin. "Yeah, I reckon I do," he said in a low voice. "Truth be told, old Chester and me are closer than brothers. Wouldn't know what to do with myself if I lost him. Reckon the day will come when I'll lose my old friend..." Billy shook his head in sadness. "Good Lord sure gives us some mighty good animals to love, but it's a shame that love can't be for a lifetime."

"Love is forever in the heart, Billy," Rita said and gently touched Billy's hand. "I'm sure Chester has many good years left in him."

Billy raised his eyes. He looked at Rita through new eyes. It felt strange having a beautiful woman offer him words of comfort and understand him so well after such a short time. After all, he was a tough man and one unaccustomed to attention...but Rita's words touched his heart and brought peace to his mind. "Yeah, I reckon Chester ain't going nowhere for a while yet."

"You bet," Rita smiled. She looked straight up at the pine tree. "This pine sure is beautiful. I love the colors of autumn but I'm always impressed how the pine tree stands alone, steadfast and green, never changing." Rita moved her eyes to Billy. "You remind me of a pine tree, Billy."

"I do?" Billy asked in a confused voice.

"Sure," Rita explained, growing more comfortable with Billy despite the blush that she couldn't seem to keep from her cheeks every time he made her laugh. Rita couldn't really put into words how talking to Billy made her feel; she knew it could mean he was a special person. "You're evergreen, you know?"

"I don't rightly understand what you mean," Billy said and scratched the back of his neck. "I reckon I ain't one of them fancy city boys with college degrees under my belt, and maybe that's why I don't understand your meaning. My daddy always said corn seed can't talk to a carburetor. Reckon I ain't nothing but a corn seed."

Rita quickly scanned the area for Rhonda. The last thing in the world she wanted was for her sister to pop up out of nowhere humming Here Comes The Bride while she tried to explain to this gentle, wonderful man exactly how special he was. "Billy, what I mean is that you're...someone with inner strength. You know who you are and you don't need to change. You understand what life is."

"Me?" Billy asked and let out a guffaw. "My daddy once told me I could live a hundred years and still be wet behind my ears," he laughed. "All I know is my farm...I sure ain't got life figured out. No ma'am, not in a million years." Billy slapped his leg in amusement.

Rita blushed. "What I meant to say is...you're a good person, Billy. You have a true heart and you don't put on a show for anyone...you're real."

Billy shook his head. "I don't think I'm that different from anyone else," he said quietly and slowly dried up his laughter. "I live with a demanding old hound dog in a big old empty farmhouse and raise crops and tend my animals. Sometimes I think Juan and José and the pumpkins know more about me than most folks in Clovedale Falls do. But shucks, that don't make me special."

Rita sighed. It was clear that Billy was a man who wasn't used to receiving compliments. "I get it, Billy," she said and thought for a moment. "I used to say the same thing when folks would thank me for my service as a police officer, or for helping them. They assumed there was nothing normal about me becoming a cop. What woman in her right mind would want to risk her life like that?" Rita shook her head. "I pride myself on being a practical woman and maybe I chose the most illogical career a woman could choose. But to me it was the only choice possible. It was what I felt called to do. I was good at it, my sister and I loved the work. It didn't make me special, it just made me willing to do the work. Does that make sense?"

"Being a cop is something to be mighty proud of," Billy told Rita.

"Really?" Rita asked. "Think about it…long hours, lousy food in your cruiser at two in the morning, dangerous criminals and more red tape than you can imagine...yeah, I'm proud of my work, but behind the scenes it's not all noble deeds and saving kittens from trees like some people think it is." Rita looked at Billy. "I've been shot at, nearly killed dozens of times, attacked, hit, spit on, and called every name in the book. And for what? To send some thug to prison who will eventually get out on parole and go right back to the streets." She laughed a little.

Billy studied Rita's slumped posture and sad eyes. "I didn't mean to make you upset. I'm mighty sorry…"

"You didn't upset me, Billy," Rita confessed, sitting up again and trying to shake the bitterness from her soul. "You just remind me of myself."

"I do?"

"I tried to compliment you and you shook it off. I do the same thing when a person tells me how great it is that I was a cop." Rita gazed toward the hospital. "I have a passion for justice, Billy, and a disgust for crime."

"That's a good way to be," Billy assured Rita. "Ain't a thing in the world wrong with a person liking justice. The good Lord tells us to seek justice."

"I know," Rita replied and slowly folded her arms. She grew silent for a minute and then said: "And there ain't a thing wrong with making a farm bloom with beauty and love. Takes a special kind of man to keep doing that the right way, the old fashioned way, day in and day out, every season and every year, for the tourists and the locals…we wouldn't have the Pumpkin Festival without local farmers like you. No one puts on a better hayride than you or a bigger corn maze. You may think it's just work, but it's important," she said quietly, gently patting his arm a few times for emphasis. "It's important, Billy."

"Uh…thank you, ma'am. I reckon I don't know what to say," Billy said. They sat together for a moment in silence, simply listening to the gentle autumn breeze as it rustled through the trees and across the hospital's trim green lawn.

"You're a good man, Billy, and I like that. You may talk to your cornfields but that's a whole lot better than city boys who talk to corrupt lawyers and crooked politicians like in my old job. I can't tell you what a breath of fresh air you are. With you I know who I'm talking to…a decent, kind, hardworking man." Rita stood up and reached out to shake his hand. "I'm glad we're friends, Billy."

Billy stood up and focused on Rita's beautiful face, shaking her hand gently with a smile dawning on his face like pure joy. When they dropped their hands he shuffled his feet a little as she turned to go back to the sheriff's car to wait for her sister. "Mind if I ask you a question?" he asked in an uneasy voice pained with embarrassment.

"Sure."

"Folks in Clovedale Falls are always talkin', you know how it is…and anyway, I thought maybe I'd just ask you directly, well…why ain't you or your sister married?" Billy asked and then braced himself for a hard slap across the face. When Rita's hand stayed at her side Billy eased forward as if he were a man walking barefoot on broken glass. "I reckon it's the rudest thing to ask, but I've been kinda wondering the same thing. I mean...and please don't take offense to this...but you two are mighty pretty."

Rita felt her cheeks turn red. "Thank you."

"Aw, shucks…my daddy said it ain't wrong for a man to pay a compliment to a pretty lady just as long as his heart is in the right place," Billy explained. "And my heart is in the right place," he hastened to add, though he seemed to stumble over his words and get embarrassed. "I mean, that is…I just meant to say—"

"Billy, it's fine," Rita laughed. "I guess neither of us ever found the right man, you could say." She tried to keep from looking into his clear, honest eyes and could hardly look away. "And thank you for the compliment. I don't mind it at all."

He swallowed nervously and sighed in relief. "Folks today seem to take offense at anything. Why, a couple of days ago I told this woman from California that she was wearing a hat...one of them ladies' sun hats I think it was." Billy shook his head, chattering away in his nervousness. "I was just being friendly and sure didn't care for the hat the woman was wearing, no sir. But she was buying a whole bunch of pumpkins and it just seemed fitting to say something nice. Boy, what a mistake that was. Why, that woman looked at me like I was rabid mule preparing to bite her."

"Sounds like a real special customer, Billy." Rita suppressed a grin.

Billy shrugged his shoulders. "Woman bought her pumpkins and ain't been back to my farm since. Good riddance, too." Billy took a second to let his eyes catch some falling leaves. "In the old days folks would come from all over the county, enjoy the festival, talk, laugh, cut a rug, and go home happy. But through the years I've seen the tourists change into...strangers. I can't really explain it. I mean, there's still plenty of mighty decent folk that come through Clovedale Falls...but they're all...the same. Same fancy cars, same clothes, same look...it's like being stuck in one of them horror movies full of clones or robots."

"I know what you mean," Rita told Billy, surprised to hear the man speaking about this on a deeper level. "Everyone drives in from all over…there's no such thing as 'local' anymore."

"Boy, you can say that again," Billy nodded his head. He shoved his hands into the front pockets of his overalls and looked down at his work boots. "Used to be a man drove up on my farm with a truck full of excited kids who understood how to say yes sir and yes ma'am. These days all you get is a bunch of smart-mouth kids with manners that'll make your stomach turn. I reckon not all kids are like that, but boy, let me tell you, I'm hogtying more and more folks these days..."

"Careful, Billy. Sheriff Bluestone might not tolerate that forever," Rita couldn't help but tease him.

Billy raised his eyebrows. "Sheriff didn't see that punk Yankee kid who pulled a knife on me! Back in my day we respected our elders," he said in a sad voice. "My daddy told me when I was no taller than a corn shoot that there's trouble when folks start locking the front doors before bedtime. Never thought I'd see the day, but now nobody is neighborly anymore and front doors seem to be locked most of the time. Never thought my eyes would see folks that seem to come right out of a deranged movie, either. Yesterday I saw this fella with green and pink hair….half of his head was shaved to boot. For a minute I thought the circus was in town."

Rita fought back a grin. In her mind she saw Billy staring at a person with green and pink hair, the gape-mouthed expression on his face as he watched, and she let a giggle slip from her mouth. "I hope you didn't hogtie him?"

"No ma'am. Why, I marched right up to him and asked if had some kind of fungus on his head," Billy stated in a serious voice.

"You didn't," Rita giggled again.

"I sure enough did. And do you know what he told me?"

"I can hardly wait to hear," Rita anxiously said.

Billy drew in a deep breath and made a strange face. "That fella told me that his head was some kind of art...that he was expressing his...what did that fella say?" Billy scratched the back of his neck, thought for a second, and then nodded his head. "Oh yeah, now I remember. That fella said that he was expressing his inner personality. Boy, if that's what his inner self looks like..." Billy whistled.

Rita laughed. "Billy, you're too much."

Billy felt his cheeks redden. "I reckon this old fella just prefers the old days."

"Me, too," Rita smiled and just then spotted Rhonda exiting through the front doors. "There's my sister, Billy," she said in a disappointed voice. "I guess it's time for me to leave."

Billy saw Rhonda, waved a friendly hand at her, and then looked at Rita. "Sure been nice talking to you," he said softly. "Reckon I better go see about Juan."

"Okay," Rita smiled and waved goodbye to Billy. She hurried over to Rhonda and climbed into the car. She gave her sister a stern, forbidding look. "Not a word out of you, miss."

"Not a word," Rhonda grinned, waved at Chester, and buckled her seatbelt.

"Well, back to the mansion," Rita said and sighed. "Back to...murder."

Rhonda stopped at the security gate. "If we were smart we would have asked Brad for the security code before we left," she told Rita.

"We had a lot on our minds," Rita said in her practical voice. "Just push the call button. I'm sure Nurse Mae will answer."

Rhonda glanced at her sister. It was clear that Rita didn't want to talk about her sweet little interlude with Billy on the bench under the pine tree. During the drive up the steep hill, Rita had been very quiet. "Brad hasn't tried to contact us the entire time we were in town. I'm assuming everything is still quiet," she told Rita, trying to focus on the tasks before them.

"Brad is a very skilled sheriff," Rita replied. "We both saw him put six bullets through the center of his target at the range. We each got the center twice—"

"No, I got three times," Rhonda said in a proud voice.

"Don't remind me…I was having an off day," Rita complained. "My point is, Miss Braggart, that Brad isn't a rookie. He's fully capable of taking care of himself. If he hasn't called us that must mean the situation is still in the green."

Rhonda shot a curious eye at Rita. "Why the sudden practical face again?" she asked. "Is anything wrong? You looked so happy when we left the hospital."

Rita studied the closed security gate and then gazed around at the delete landscape, searched for the river, and then sighed. "I was feeling okay when we left Billy, but then I began thinking about something he said...about the tourists."

"What?" Rhonda asked.

Rita gazed across at some trees and through her open window heard a woodpecker start knocking at a tree. "Billy said the tourists are changing," she finally spoke. "The people driving through Clovedale Falls aren't all friendly locals like they were back when Billy was a young boy and his father ran the Northfield Farm."

"I wouldn't think so," Rhonda replied. "It's been decades since then, why wouldn't times change? It can't stay the nineteen-fifties forever. However…it would be really cool to see the fairgrounds filled with 1957 Corvettes. Guys wearing letterman jackets and gals wearing circle skirts below their knees. Kids excited over ten-cent hotdogs and can roam free all the time…parents who still sit down at the dinner table with their children at night."

"Exactly," Rita pointed out. "The mindset has changed, Rhonda...and there's no denying that crime has increased along with it." Rita felt her heart become heavy. "We have retired and the world is no safer. Each day this world grows more and more dangerous." Rita nodded her head toward the gate. "Even way up here…a woman was murdered. And look at us, two sisters who only want a peaceful early retirement...and we're stuck investigating another murder. Why? Because people like Noel and Beth wanted a quick paycheck. People are growing more and more cruel by the day."

Rhonda heard the heaviness in her sister's voice. "Honey, that's just life. We can't stop time and we can't despair. We can't hope to change the hearts of all people. All we can do is fight back and protect the people and the places we love. Sure, I hate being back on another murder case as much as you do, but the fact of the matter is Brad needs our help and, well, justice is more important than strolling around a Pumpkin Festival sipping hot apple cider."

Rita focused back on the river. "Sitting on that bench under the pine tree…it got me thinking about what it might be like to…marry Billy," she confessed. "Now, before you go haywire on me, let me explain—"

"Please do," Rhonda begged, her eyes wide with surprise.

"I don't want to marry Billy…I simply needed to…create a scenario in my mind," Rita explained, aiming for a practical tone of voice and failing just a little. "What if Billy and I got married and had a child."

"A child…okay…" Rhonda said. She could see the fondness in her twin sister's eyes and did not wish to spoil the moment by teasing her. Perhaps Rita was not yet ready to admit the depth of her feelings for Billy. "Just hypothetically, right?"

Rita nodded her head as her eyes watched the river sparkling through the trees. "If Billy and I had a child," she continued, "what future would that child have in a world torn apart by people who are determined to…hate one another? Would I really want my child to follow in our footsteps? Think about it…a child could become a cop and defend the ideas of corrupt politicians…or become a small business farmer and deal with the crushing weight of policies set by the blind idiots in the state and federal government? It sounds like a life of despair and bankruptcy. Or would I want my child to join a military that no longer defends our nation but serves as a bully force for political aims around the world in never-ending wars?" Rita looked at Rhonda in distress. "I know I sound radical, but when you break it down and truly explore the details, there's all this dirt swept under the rug and I can't ignore it anymore."

"I know, honey," Rhonda agreed. "I have eyes to see."

Rita looked down to her lap, fiddling with her nails. "My child could become a doctor...a nurse...something in the healthcare profession, I suppose. Someplace they could try to make a difference, to help people. I'm not implying all hope is lost. But the fight...my goodness, what a fight it would be to be a light in this dark world." Rita firmly settled her hands in her lap before she could do any more damage to her poor cuticles. "Then there's Billy," she said, looking up at her sister with true confusion and fear in her eyes. "If Billy wasn't a farmer who owned his land...what would he do, Rhonda? Where would a man like Billy truly fit in today's world?"

"I...never thought about that," Rhonda confessed. "I guess he wouldn't fit in anywhere. He'd have to retrain for a different job…though I can't see him liking that very much…"

"Exactly my point," Rita agreed. "The only way he survives is by remaining practical about keeping to his work at the farm. Marriage and a child would honestly be a mistake...a joke...and there's no room for jokes in a practical life. I firmly believe that. The practicality is key. Why? Because a man can't even tell a woman she's wearing a nice hat without being made to feel like a viral disease..."

"Rita, what are you talking about?"

Rita sighed and buried her face in her hands.

We can't stop smiling," she told Rita and patted her hand. "Rita, the day we stop smiling is the day the enemy wins."

Rita shook her head and looked up. "The day my child is forced to hunker down and accept corruption in order to live...the day Billy has to teach his child to hogtie someone who has threatened his life...isn't the enemy already winning?"

"Don't say that," Rhonda said forcefully. "You've never given up the good fight and you're not about to start now. Yeah, it might be true that Billy has to hogtie some unruly tourist, but that's always been the case. You're making a mountain out of a molehill. If the world is truly getting uglier by the day...shouldn't it be our mission to bring a little bit more beauty to our corner of the world? As long as there are people like you and me fighting the good fight...and people like Billy and Brad...Mark and Erma and all our new friends here...well, life still has a cherry on top."

Rita pointed to the mansion beyond the gate. "And life still has murders."

Rhonda shrugged her shoulders. "Murder is going to happen no matter when or where in the world we live. And besides, we chose our profession. No one forced us to walk those dark alleys. We're the ones with years of training in this town. We're the ones who can make a difference here. We could fall into despair and walk away at any time but how does that solve the problem? If you're going to make a mountain out of a molehill, at least keep climbing the mountain with me."

"I don't know. I guess I'm just tired of climbing the mountain only to find out it's been a trash heap all along and there's only rats waiting at the top," Rita sighed.

"My, you are depressed," Rhonda said and shook her head.

"Why shouldn't I be?" Rita asked. "My hypothetical husband is a farmer who is laughed at by the world and my future child is forced to fight in vain against the forces of evil and hatred..."

"Honey..." Rhonda started to speak and then stopped. Arguing with Rita when she was in a sour mood was pointless. "Okay, let's focus on the case," she said and quickly pushed a call button on the security box. "But listen, just because you're depressed doesn't undo the fact that you were blushing like a schoolgirl under that pine tree. There isn't a single thing you could say that will convince me otherwise," Rhonda said in a fierce yet kind voice. Just as Rita was about to make an angry retort, the gate simply started to open. "That's strange," Rhonda said. "No one answered me."

Rita bent forward and snatched her gun free from her ankle holster, the argument quickly forgotten. "Okay," she said in a quick voice, "I'll go in on foot. You drive the car up to the mansion, park, and circle around to the back door. I'll search the land down by the river and meet you around back if the coast is clear."

"Got it," Rhonda said without a moment's hesitation.

Rita nodded her head, jumped out of the car, and waited for Rhonda to drive through the gate. Once Rhonda was clear of the gate she made her way off the road and began working her way around the foot of the hill under the shadows of the copse of trees. The beautiful landscape loomed like a dark battleground around her, hiding unseen dangers and perilous traps. "Okay, Brad," she whispered, staying close to the river, searching the land with skilled eyes, "what's happening up there?"

As Rita sprinted along through the woods, Rhonda drove up to the front of the mansion and parked as if nothing was wrong. She got out, stretched her arms, looked around, and then casually strolled around to the back door. "I can feel eyes on me," she whispered, the hair standing up on the back of her neck. "I know you're there."

A dark figure watched from a third floor window as Rhonda walked up to the back door, paused, and looked around, focusing on the nearby bench in the flower garden instead of heading into the kitchen. "Where is your sister?" the voice hissed. "Why aren't you going in?"

Rhonda made her way to the bench, sat down, pretending that she was bored. Down in the woods, Rita continued to check around, moving from one tree to the next, surveying the mansion from all sides, studying the windows, searching for surveilling eyes or clues to what was going on inside. The glare from the sunlight on the river flashed up onto the windows and she could not see anything through them.

"At least the grounds seem to be clear," she whispered, standing behind a tall oak tree. "Something must be going on inside..." Rita grew silent and listened to the voice of her gut—the voice all cops depend on. "The killer is inside," she whispered. "The killer is expecting us." Rita checked her gun safety with uneasy eyes. "Brad and Mae must be in danger...what choice do I have?" she asked and hurried up the little hill to find Rhonda at the back door.

When Rhonda saw Rita approaching at a near sprint, she immediately understood her sister's intentions. "We have a game to play, don't we," she said.

Rita nodded her head. "Whoever is inside is expecting us."

The dark figure moved to a different window and spotted Rita and Rhonda conferring below. "Quit delaying. You came up empty handed," the figure hissed. The women's conversation stretched on far too long. The figure reached out, unlocked the window, and slowly pulled it open, and then yelled: "If you want your friends to live, do as I say!"

Rita and Rhonda shot their heads upward and spotted a man wearing a thick gray sweatshirt with the hood pulled up and cinched tight over the head. A black handkerchief was tied in front of the face, blocking the man's features, leaving only his eyes visible. "Put your guns down now or I'll shoot your friends before you can reach them."

"Mid to early fifties," Rhonda whispered as she held her hands up in the air.

"Russian accent," Rita whispered back, keeping her arms low but her hands visible.

"It all fits," Rita nodded her head and took a chance. She yelled upward to the open window, "Anton Peterson? We'll put our weapons down." It could be none other than Rusty's adopted nephew, the one his brother had adopted and had later fled back to Russia seeking his birth family.

"Put down your guns!" Anton yelled from the third floor window he was standing at. "How do you know my name?"

"Anton, we just want to talk," Rita tried.

"Put down the weapons now!"

"Okay, okay," Rhonda cautiously squatted down, took her gun from the holster attached to her ankle, and tossed it into a soft patch of grass. Rita hesitated and then tossed her gun next to Rhonda's. "Still have your backup?" she whispered.

"Afraid not," Rhonda whispered back in a miserable voice.

"I didn't put my backup in my purse today either," Rita sighed.

"Why would we?" Rhonda asked, raising her eyes up to the window again, "We were supposed to have a fun day at the festival, remember?"

Rita lifted her eyes and saw Anton glaring down at her. As she did, the back door burst open. A woman in her mid-fifties appeared and pointed a gun at Rita and Rhonda. "Inside," the woman snapped in a thick German accent. The woman scooped up Rita and Rhonda's guns and pointed to the kitchen inside. "Now!"

Rita soaked in the details of the woman before she turned to go inside. The woman wore a black jogging suit, and Rita quickly memorized the style of her short grayish-blonde hair, and her thin, boney, facial features and cruel, pale blue eyes. "Who are you?" she asked, delaying for time.

"Inside," the woman hissed, "my husband is not a very patient man."

"Inside, now!" Anton yelled from above once more. "Do as Lara orders or your friends will die!"

Lara pointed the gun she was holding at Rhonda and clicked off the safety. "Inside or you die here! Makes no difference to me."

"Okay...okay," Rita said and tossed her hands up. "We're going inside...just take it easy."

Rhonda looked deep into the woman's pale, blank eyes and saw nothing more than a deep, empty hole; a woman who possessed no conscience or concern for mankind—a true killer. Yet she was not afraid. "Is there any coffee I can have?" she asked Lara as they were marched into the kitchen with the gun at their backs.

"Shut up!"

"Never hurts to ask," Rhonda said and nudged Rita with her elbow. "Take it easy," she whispered. "We need to play this carefully."

"I was about to tell you the same thing," Rita whispered back as they walked into the kitchen. Brad and Mae were sitting at the kitchen table with their hands behind their backs, locked tightly in handcuffs.

"I would say hello," Rita said, walking toward the table, "but from all the duct tape over your mouths I take it our new friends don't want us talking much." Lara shoved Rita a little bit forward and she stumbled and caught herself against the edge.

Rhonda spotted Brad and Mae and shook her head. Whoever Anton was, she thought, he surely had some skill. It wasn't easy to take down a man like Sheriff Brad Bluestone. And speaking of Brad, she thought, looking at the sheriff's furious face, he was obviously hungering to avenge himself. Over the cruelly tight duct tape the sheriff's skin was reddened and his eyes were dark with anger. "Well, we're one big happy family now," she said as

Lara slammed the back door shut and engaged the deadbolt.

"Sit," Lara ordered and motioned at the two other chairs at the kitchen table. Rita looked at Rhonda and sat down. Rhonda shrugged her shoulders and plopped down next to Mae.

"We should have handled this differently," Rita muttered in a miserable voice.

"What choice did we have?" Rhonda asked in a hushed tone. "One woman is dead...hostages are involved...and we don't exactly have a professional SWAT team in town."

"Shut up," Lara snapped. She aimed her gun at Mae. "One more word and she's dead."

Rita and Rhonda both looked into Lara's eyes. The woman meant her words. Mae, knowing full well that Lara would shoot her without a moment's hesitation, begged Rita and Rhonda with her eyes. Rita nodded her head and looked toward the walk-in freezer. The padlock was missing. Rhonda noticed and began wondering what Anton and his terrifying wife had done with poor Lynn Hogan's body. She was afraid to find out. But Rhonda did know that whatever was taking place had to do with money...and a very unfortunate old man named Rusty Lowly was caught in the middle of a sick game.

8

Anton walked into the kitchen with a dangerous, powerful swagger that told Rita and Rhonda the man had no compunctions about killing his hostages regardless of how the situation turned out. "I want to thank you for getting rid of those annoying cooks," he said without removing his hood or the handkerchief covering his face. "I don't mind murder…but the fewer squawking idiots the better."

"What do you want?" Rhonda asked, pretending to play dumb. She needed to get Anton talking and fast.

Anton reached into the front pocket of his baggy black pants, pulled out a pair of handcuffs, and ordered Rita to hold up her left wrist. "Put these on and then cuff your wrist to your sister's right wrist." He trained a gun on them and Lara held her aim on the sisters as well.

"Do it!" Lara growled.

Rita shot Rhonda a worried look. Rhonda shrugged her shoulders. "Do it," she said, "what other choice do we have?"

Rita studied her sister's eyes and saw something curious. "Okay," she said and Anton slung the handcuffs to Rita for her to catch. Rita hesitantly did as Anton had ordered. "There," she said, "happy?" Lara reached over and clamped down on each handcuff, making sure they were locked tight against the skin.

"For now," Anton told Rita in a cold voice. Now that the sisters were secured with handcuffs, he lowered his weapon for a moment to reach up and slowly remove his handkerchief, revealing a stone cold face to match his eyes. A long scar ran down his right cheek, dark and crooked on his rough skin. "Better," he said and tossed the handkerchief down onto the kitchen table. "Lara, check the old people. I locked them in but we can't be too careful."

Lara looked at Rita and Rhonda with a vicious warning in her eyes and then hurried out of the kitchen without a word.

"My wife isn't much for talk," Anton explained, his Russian accent apparent. "But she is a woman that a man like myself can depend on."

"I bet," Rhonda said in a sarcastic voice. "You get along like a house on fire...perfect."

Anton walked in front of Rhonda and glared at her. "The women you drove away from here spoke too much. I should have killed them when I had the chance but I was… unavoidably detained."

"Detained?" Rita asked.

"Detained," Anton grinned, crossed over to the walk-in freezer, and yanked the door open. "Out!" he yelled.

Kathy Stein burst out of the freezer, shaking all over and her skin almost blue, her hands tied behind her back. Her mouth was duct-taped shut but her terrified eyes blurted out everything Rita and Rhonda needed to know.

"Oh, I see," Rhonda said, "you went and found yourself a friend."

"A useless friend," Anton grinned and motioned with his gun for Kathy to stand still. "A dead friend, maybe. This woman refuses to cooperate with me. She claims she knows nothing of the money." Anton turned his attention to Mae. "You, nurse. I heard you speaking to Kathy about the Hogan woman's money." Anton grinned. "I have listening devices everywhere. While you talk, I plan. While you sleep, I prowl."

"Get to the point," Rita snapped at Anton. "We don't want to sit here and listen to you brag."

Anton frowned. "Don't speak to me that way," he warned Rita. "I am a man with pride."

"Just get to the point," Rhonda said to Anton and then pointed accusingly at Kathy. Kathy lowered her eyes. "Don't play the victim with us, sister," Rhonda said. "You may look pretty in that fancy department store outfit and that blonde salon hairstyle when you go out with your rich friends wearing your best diamonds, but we know that underneath that lovely face of makeup is nothing more than a monster."

Kathy's head drooped down and her shoulders heaved as if she was crying. Anton tutted with a total lack of sympathy. "Now, now. Aren't we all monsters?" Anton asked.

"No," Rhonda told Anton in a voice that caused his cheeks to turn red. "But I wouldn't expect you to understand that. There are people who would casually poison an old man to manipulate him," she spit her words in Kathy's direction with no remorse. "And then there are people in this life who are good, who stand for justice."

"You're an idiot if you believe that," Anton hissed at Rhonda. He pointed his gun at her and narrowed his eyes. "All cops are monsters," he said and fingered the scar on his cheek. "All cops are monsters and this world is nothing but garbage..."

Rhonda looked over at her sister Rita, and saw that Rita was struggling to contain her horror and depression at the oddly familiar words coming out of Anton's mouth. "Look," Rhonda said quickly in a wise-guy voice. "this is America, pal. I'm sorry for whatever happened to you, and maybe in Russia you would get away with this kind of angst, but here the drama is getting to be a little bit much. Can we stop with the scar stroking and just get on with the show?"

"The show is about to end for all of you unless that woman tells me what I want to know," Anton snapped. "My patience is running very thin." Anton walked over to Kathy and ripped the duct tape off her mouth. Kathy let out a frightened scream and began to beg Anton for her life. "Shut up," Anton ordered. "Be quiet."

Kathy jerked her eyes at Mae. "Please, help me…this madman thinks Mrs. Hogan left me her money. I tried to tell him that all of her money will go to a charity after she dies…you have to help me make him understand…"

"Liar!" Anton yelled. "I heard your friend the nurse here talking to you about the Hogan money. I heard her tell you Mrs. Hogan was going to leave all her money to you."

"Ah, so that's when you came up with the plan to kill the poor woman, right?" Rhonda asked. "The blackmail money you were receiving from Kathy Stein wasn't enough, right?" Mae looked shocked at Rhonda's words and behind her duct tape her expression went dead white with fear and dread.

Anton swung his attention back to Rhonda. "Blackmail? Small potatoes. Never mind all that. I'm taking this mansion," he said in a careless voice that sent a chill down Rhonda's back. "Lots of rich people here…lots of money to steal. But first I need the big money. You think I am a criminal…no, no. You have me all wrong." He stood up straighter and unzipped his sweatshirt, revealing his neatly pressed shirt and suit vest underneath. "I am just a businessman." His smile was cold and calculating and evil. "And a businessman needs money to hire medical, house and grounds staff. I need money to pay expenses and transform this mansion into a booming business."

"And a little crime to season the soup, right?" Rhonda asked. "What are you planning? Are you going to hide an underground betting parlor down in the basement? Run guns, drugs, dirty money? All while stealing dough from innocent people…."

Anton grabbed Kathy's arm and pushed her toward the kitchen table. "That's right," he said, "but none of you will be alive to stop me. I'm going to turn this sleepy little town into a gold mine for my friends back in Russia." Anton felt his scar again.

"You mean your mafia friends?" Rhonda said.

He seemed not to hear her. "I'm going to show all of them...every one of them...Anton Peterson is a man you can cut down, but he fights back." Anton lowered his hand. "Once I get the cash I need...I'll show them."

Kathy moved close to Mae, cowering in fear. "Anton, I don't know what you heard Mae telling me, but you obviously heard her wrong," she pleaded in a voice that was used to being spoiled—a voice filled with contempt and condescension. "Lynn Hogan did speak with Mae about her money and asked Mae to be sure that her money went to medical research after she died and I'm sorry if you misunderstood—"

"Don't lie to me!" Anton warned Kathy. "Pitiful woman. I heard your friend tell you she wanted to leave all of her money to you."

Kathy eased as close to Mae as possible. Mae looked up at her with sour eyes. "Oh please, Mae, don't look at me like that," Kathy begged. "You don't understand...I had to..."

"Had to what?" Rita asked. "Steal an innocent old man's memories? Kill an old woman?"

"You don't understand," Kathy begged. "I can't lose this mansion...it belonged to my mother...it was all going to fall apart...I made a promise—"

"Oh, can it," Rhonda yelled at Kathy, finally losing her temper. "Maybe your mother had a heart of gold but you sure don't. You can't keep a sweet promise in a heart filled with vinegar, sister."

"That's not true," Kathy insisted as mascara-stained tears spilled from her eyes. "I loved my mother...I loved...I love...this mansion. Perhaps I let myself fall into a little bit of trouble, but—"

"You sent a woman to poison an innocent man. You sent someone to erase the memories of a man who lived his life protecting innocent people," Rita told Kathy in a disgusted voice. "You crossed a red line."

"You don't understand," Kathy begged. "That stupid high school kid messed up everything for me...if only he hadn't contacted Anton…"

"If only," Anton said with a wry little humorless smirk. "You shut up, now," he said, aiming his weapon at Kathy for emphasis. "That kid did me a favor. I was down to my last dime and thanks to his innocent little 'interview request' I was able to connect the dots back to you…and finally get some of the money I am owed. Or at least, enough cash from you to be able to clear my thoughts and plan my future." Anton looked at the kitchen door. "Lara and I were living in Los Angeles in a run-down apartment no better than a closet." Anton kept his eyes on the door as if he was afraid Lara might hear him, or the past might reach out and snatch him back. "I was breaking my back as a filthy mechanic… working on anything I could find…every day for years…" Anton felt his scar again. "I had to flee Russia like a coward…and I could no longer do the business work I was accustomed to. I was forced to become a common worker…live in grease and poverty like a rat." He advanced on Kathy with every word.

"Please—" Kathy begged.

"Shut up!" Anton ordered. "You threatened that high school student for asking questions. What did he do except expose you for what you really are? A spoiled, rich brat who used her position to get away with her crimes. To keep a house that should not belong to her. Who is the mafia here, me or you? If the tables were turned, that student would be on a pedestal for exposing a criminal. Stop whining and accept your lot."

Kathy stared at Anton. "I can get you more money," she promised in a shaky voice. "Please…don't kill me. I have children…and a husband…and—"

"I want Lynn Hogan's money," Anton snapped at Kathy. "Give me the money and turn this property over to me and I will let you live."

"He's lying," Rhonda warned Kathy.

Kathy bowed her head. "Anton, I've already told you over and over that I have no control over Mrs. Hogan's money. For crying out loud….if I did...do you think I would be hiring high school kids to take care of the grounds? Do you honestly think I wouldn't have paid off my gambling debt by now? Use your brains for crying out loud and think!"

Rita and Rhonda quickly glanced at each other. Rita nodded her head. "Anton," Rhonda said, "Kathy is telling you the truth. You may not believe her, but she is." Rhonda looked over at Kathy, shook her head in disgust, and then focused back on Anton. "You can go ahead and kill all of us but you're not going to get any money out of the deal."

"You killed Lynn Hogan for nothing," Rita added.

"Killed?" Anton asked in a surprised voice. "I didn't kill Lynn Hogan and neither did Lara. Rusty Lowly killed her."

"No he didn't," Rita snapped. "Don't you dare blame that woman's death on that innocent man, do you hear me?"

We needed the old woman alive to sign over the money." Anton raised his hand at Kathy whose tears fell fast and messy. "Do you think I am an idiot like this blubbering fool? You think I would ruin everything like that? No."

Rhonda looked at Rita. "I hate to admit it, but I think this skunk is telling the truth."

"Skunk is right," Rita said and waved her free hand in front of her face. "Brush your teeth...stinky."

Anton leaned up from Rita. "That old man killed Lynn Hogan," he said, unbothered. "I heard Mae tell that sheriff of yours that he was found in her room holding the knife." Anton looked at Brad. "All you had to do was follow the rules and I would have laid low for a while until the air cleared. I was surprised...and pleased...when Lara told me you were diving into the deep end...alone...with only two life jackets to depend on." Anton grinned at the twins. "Killing three small town cops is a lot easier than killing a Fed. Small town cops get very little mention on the news but a Fed is painted all over the news like some kind of hero."

Rita focused on Brad's face. Brad's eyes were locked on Anton in battle mode. "Look," she said, "it's clear that Kathy Stein has no control over Mrs. Hogan's money. The only woman who does is dead. So what are you going to do now? Why even keep us alive?"

Anton gritted his teeth, marched up to Mae, and ripped the duct tape off her mouth. "Tell them! Tell them what you said. You must know something more. I heard you tell Kathy that…" he yelled.

Mae flinched. "You...heard me talking to a woman named Kathy...but it wasn't Kathy Stein," Mae confessed in a shaky voice. "Lynn Hogan did originally tell Kathy Stein her money was going to be left to a medical research charity...but..." Mae paused. If she confessed her secret it would surely make everyone hate her. But, she thought, she really had nothing to hide. "I haven't broken any laws," she insisted weakly.

"Mae, what are you talking about?" Rhonda asked in a caring voice. "Talk to us...and...trust us, Mae. Please."

Mae looked into Rhonda's eyes. The woman had earned her trust, which was very rare. "I have a daughter," she told Rhonda and then looked at Rita, pleading. "My daughter has Down Syndrome and lives in a special community." Mae drew in a deep breath. "Not even Kathy knows about my daughter."

"Mae, why didn't you tell—" Kathy began to speak.

"Some secrets are best kept silent," Mae told Kathy. "I... named my daughter after your mother. I named her after my beloved Miss Katherine. I loved your mother very much and respected her as my dearest and closest friend. Your mother helped me through a horrible divorce and began paying for my daughter to go to a special school. It was your mother, Kathy, who begged me to keep my daughter a secret from the world."

"Why?" Rita asked.

Mae drew in another deep breath. "Miss Katherine was so afraid my husband might come back and try to take her away from me," Mae explained. "He was a cruel man, the kind who would get a judge in his corner and get my daughter locked up in a cheap state facility in no time at all. She'd never survive there." She looked at Kathy with sour resentment on her face like a stain. "I was able to pay for her living community until you started stealing from the books. Oh, how I wanted to believe that you were innocent, Kathy...I wanted to defend you, protect you...I wanted to believe the goodness that lived in your mother lived on inside of you. I was wrong...and because of you...each month I was left practically penniless." Mae looked at Rita and Rhonda. "I'm sorry I bent the truth a little...you must understand, I had my daughter to protect."

"But why speak of your daughter now?" Rita asked confused and looked at Anton. "Why now?"

Mae locked eyes with Anton. "Lynn was a lovely lady...she had a heart of gold. One day, for no reason, I showed her a photo of my daughter. She had seen me crying on Mother's Day and thought, wrongly, that I had lost a little one long ago. I explained that my daughter was very much alive, but I had my fears of losing her. I was assured me that I would never lose my daughter and secretly arranged to begin paying for her monthly expenses...I only found out when the billing department sent back my check. That was about three months ago—"

"What are you saying," Anton snapped, his eyes widening as he started to put the pieces together.

"My point is," Mae snapped back, "you're not getting a dime. You heard me talking to Kathy about Lynn's money, but it wasn't Kathy Stein. It was my daughter, Katherine Taylor. And don't get any ideas, because I've spoken to Lynn's estate attorney and let me assure you it's all arranged…her accounts will stay as they currently are and no one is getting a dime." Mae shook her head at Anton. "You might as well kill us now and take this mansion, but as far as money goes? All you're getting today is fool's gold."

Anton didn't like the news Mae had splattered him in the face with. His cheeks grew redder than cayenne pepper. He had intended on Kathy Stein staying alive to manage his new crooked business ventures. But now, the idea of leaving behind so many witnesses no longer sat well in his gut. Nor could he kill them all without money to escape. It would be an empty act with no reward involved. Anton knew he couldn't leave five witnesses alive, yet the thought of killing them all for nothing made him ill—it was too much to clean up and he barely had enough money in the bank to get through the week. "Listen, woman," he threatened Mae, "I'll find that daughter of yours and make her suffer!"

"You'll never find my daughter," Mae promised Anton. "My daughter lives under a fake name in another state. I hid her well so my ex-husband would never find her. She lives in a community that is so private that only the Secret Service can locate it." Mae looked deep into Anton's eyes. "You'll never get a penny of Mrs. Hogan's money," she said in a satisfied voice. "I may die today but I'll die knowing that once Lynn's death is cleared up all of her money will go to my daughter."

Rita and Rhonda felt a sweet love form in their hearts for Mae. The old nurse was surely holding her ground and putting a criminal in his place—a criminal, they both realized, that had not thought out his game plan very well. In fact, the sisters each realized, Anton's plan was so full of holes that they were surprised the man had even managed to blackmail Kathy without tripping over himself. It was clear that Anton was not the brains of the operation. It had to be someone else.

"Lara," Rhonda whispered.

"What?" Anton snapped.

"I said it's always a woman doing the heavy lifting, isn't it. You didn't think out your plan very well, did you?" Rhonda said. She nodded over at Kathy. "Even if Mrs. Hogan had left all of her money to Kathy Stein, how in the world were you expecting to get it? Do you know how much legal red tape is involved with a death, never mind a homicide, especially when that person is loaded with cash? Kathy knows. Her husband is a lawyer. You can't just demand millions and get them the next day." Next, Rhonda turned to focus on Kathy. "You understand the law very well, don't you Mrs. Stein. That's why you've been playing the blackmailer, stringing him along with a line of cash until you could figure out a way to get him off your back." Kathy looked horrified.

"And when you were approached about Lynn's money," Rita continued for Rhonda, "you saw a way to rid yourself of a rat, didn't you?"

"But honestly…I didn't know anything about the money," Kathy insisted, aghast.

"How were you planning to kill him, Kathy? My guess is you were planning to lure him to this mansion and kill him, right?" Rita asked.

"I—" Kathy began to speak.

Rita shook her head. "But not alone...no," she said in a curious voice and focused her eyes on Rhonda. "The wife?" she asked. The sheriff and Mae looked truly confused.

Rhonda nodded her head. "Has to be."

"What are you two talking about?" Anton demanded. He pointed his gun at Rita. "No tricks! You know I don't care if you live or die."

Rita glanced toward the doorway, saw that it was empty, and then shook her head. "Lara is hiding inside the mansion," she told Rhonda and then looked at Mae. "Mae, did you know?" she asked in a miserable voice.

"No," Mae confirmed, picking up Rita's heart and softly kissing it, "I didn't know the woman was inside the mansion. I promise."

Rhonda looked up into Anton's face and quickly slapped him with a piece of news that would surely put doubt into his heart. "How well do you trust your wife?" she asked with a small smile.

"What?" Anton asked.

Rhonda tossed her free thumb at Kathy. "Tell him, Kathy. If you don't, we will."

Kathy froze in shock. Then, as if she was a piece of ice thrown out into a desert, her face slowly began to melt in tears and an agonizing rictus of remorse. "Okay, okay… I've been having secret talks with Lara," she confessed. "Lara and I…came up with a scheme of sorts." Kathy lowered her eyes down to Mae. "Oh Mae, I'm so sorry…I needed the money."

"What are you talking about?" Mae demanded.

Kathy began to cry. "I've always known about your daughter…mother told me about her before she died," Kathy bowed her head in shame. "Lara knew that your daughter stood in the way of the whole plan…so she told me I would have to force you into giving up the money by…threatening your daughter…"

"My Lara? No," Anton said, his face darkening.

"Yes," Kathy insisted. "And she said she would do it after she killed you, Anton."

"Why you…" Mae's face exploded in rage. "I'll tear you apart with my bare hands."

"Please," Kathy begged, "I was so desperate…I wasn't going to really let Lara harm your daughter. I only wanted her to kill Anton…that's why I was poisoning Rusty Lowly, because I thought he knew the blackmailer but I had no proof." Kathy looked at Anton. "I thought Rusty's distant relations found out about his connection to the

Stonewell money…I thought I was going to lose the mansion any day…Lara was my only hope. Lara told me you were coming and I should let you kidnap me."

"What?" Anton roared.

"Lara ordered you to bring me here, Anton. It was all a trap. She panicked when Lynn Hogan was found dead… that part wasn't supposed to happen until much, much later…so Lara refused to wait any longer," Kathy blurted out. "These cops got in the way…Noel and Beth got dragged off to the jail and couldn't help us here at the mansion...the plan was so perfect. I had it all figured out." Kathy let her tears fall, playing the victim. "And then you showed up with Lara...demanding money from me, claiming you heard Mae speaking to me on the phone, throwing me in the freezer. That's when I knew I was the wrong Kathy." Kathy Stein stopped and laughed bitterly. "And Lara didn't even care. All along, Mae had been speaking to her daughter about the money and not me. I was the wrong Kathy." Kathy looked toward the kitchen door. "I could tell Lara doesn't love you, Anton...that woman is in this game for the money. So I went to Lara and played on her weak spot...and won."

"Kill all of your opponents in one shot, huh?" Rhonda asked. "Even Noel and Beth, right?"

Kathy bowed her head in shame. "Lara agreed to kill everyone involved…Rusty, Anton, Beth, Noel...and Mae," she confessed. "She promised to keep me totally out of it…in exchange for money...more money than Anton could ever give her."

"You're lying!" Anton hollered. He ran to the doorway and yelled: "Lara! Lara, get down to the kitchen right now!"

"I have a hidden key in my gun holster," Rhonda quickly whispered to Rita. "We have to get our hands free."

"I know," Rita whispered back in a worried voice. "I have a bad feeling Lara Peterson is about to clean house. Our time is short."

Rhonda saw that Anton's back was turned, and without wasting a second wedged her free hand down into the holster and began searching for the spare handcuff key she kept hidden. "There," she whispered, finding the golden treasure, and yanked her hand back up just as Anton turned around. "Any luck?" she asked.

"Shut up!" Anton yelled at Rhonda. He ran to Kathy and grabbed her by the arm. "Back into the freezer! Now!"

"Please," Kathy begged, "it's too cold, I'll freeze! We can talk, Anton...I can help you get Lynn's money from Mae…"

"Shut your lying mouth," Anton snapped and shoved Kathy back into the freezer and closed the door. As he did, someone knocked loudly on the back door. Everyone in the kitchen froze in shock, instantly silent.

"Hello?" Mark Bricker's voice called out through the door. "It's Mark, from the paper. I'm here to do a story on the house like I promised. Sorry I'm late…my car ran out of gas…you know how the gas station gets a long line during the Pumpkin Festival with all the tourists…"

"Mark?" Rhonda whispered. "But how?" Rita shrugged her shoulders.

Anton rushed to the back door and prepared his gun. "Who is this guy?" he demanded in a hoarse whisper. "Tell me or he's dead."

"Mark Bricker...he's just a local reporter," Rhonda explained in a quick voice. "He's harmless…just a skinny kid…wouldn't hurt a fly." She failed to mention that he was over six feet of wiry muscle, and crossed her fingers and prayed that Mark would not do anything stupid when the door opened.

"I forgot all about him," Mae told Anton, desperately trying to help. "I told him I wanted a story on the retirement home…for the festival." She smiled, barely concealing her fear and anxiety below the surface as Anton scowled at her.

As Mae struggled to help Rhonda with Anton's attention was diverted elsewhere, Brad worked his hands against the handcuffs holding him hostage. Lara had slapped the handcuffs on him but had failed to properly secure the latch tight enough. The left cuff had been left just loose enough to squeeze his hand through. However, the task of squeezing his hand out of the cuff while being watched was proving to be very difficult.

"Nurse Mae?" Mark knocked and called out again, confused but carefree. "Are you in there? I could have sworn her office was back here," they heard him muttering. Then again louder he continued, "I can come back later if this is a bad time?"

"Answer him," Anton said in an angry whisper. The last thing in the world he wanted was another dead fish on the menu, but what choice did he have?

Mae sighed. "I'm here, Mark!" she called out shakily.

Mark looked down at the strong stick he held in his right hand. He surely wasn't a hero, but a mansion full of elderly people and at least two beautiful women were in peril and Mark Bricker wasn't going to back down like a coward. Besides, if he lived to see another day...wow, what a story he could write! "Great! Why don't you come out to the garden when you have a second, Mae. It's too pretty of a day to interview you inside," he yelled back.

Mae looked at Anton. Anton gritted his teeth. "Get him inside or else," he ordered.

Mae nervously bit down on her lip and watched Anton disengage the deadbolt on the back door. "Mark...I'm a little under the weather. I'm afraid you're going to have to come inside."

Mark heard the deadbolt *click*, stepped away from the back door, and waited his heart racing. When no bad guy appeared he licked his lips and glanced through the doorway, but could see no one immediately. *I'm a dead man if I walk through that door,* he thought to himself and tried to strategize. *What would Clark Kent do?* he wondered and then called out: "Mae, hope you don't mind, but I saw the sheriff's car parked out front and remembered a couple of his deputies know some of the retired folks who live here…so I called the deputies to come up here. I want to get a group photo." Mark winced. Yeah, he had called for backup after crawling out of the trunk of Brad's car—the trunk he had been hiding in since the hospital parking lot, while Rhonda was inside and Rita was distracted by Billy. However, he knew backup might not be rushing onto the scene anytime soon. "Is that okay, Mae?" he asked hoping his words would spook the bad guy. "I mean, the sheriff is around, isn't he?"

Mae felt relief wash through her heart. She saw the same relief wash through Rita and Rhonda's heart. "Yes, Mark, that's fine….a group photo sounds lovely. And, yes, the sheriff is around."

Anton stomped the floor. "Idiot," he said through gritted teeth, and then nearly yanked the back door off its hinges, stormed outside through the short passageway, and aimed his gun at Mark. "Inside!" he yelled.

"Now," Rita said and Rhonda jammed the spare key into the handcuff, freed her sister, and then freed herself. "Free Brad, too."

Rhonda hurried over to Brad and got him loose just as he managed to slip his left hand free. "Easy," she whispered and pulled the duct tape off his mouth.

"Anton's mine." Brad jumped to his feet, went to the doorway, eased behind it, and waited for Anton to march his new prisoner inside.

Outside, Mark dropped his stick, raised his hands, and

nervously walked into the kitchen. "Hey ladies," he said in a sheepish voice. "Uh...so much for playing the hero."

"You still might get your chance," Rhonda winked at Mark and then smiled at Anton. "Hey, we're free, come and get us!" she yelled and dashed out of the kitchen with Rita at her side.

"What...no!" Anton yelled. He shoved Mark down onto the floor and began to give chase. He managed to take four steps before Brad exploded out from behind the kitchen door, dived at Anton's waist, and tackled the man down. "Get his gun, Mark!" Brad yelled.

"Huh...oh, yeah," Mark said in a scared but excited voice. He crawled over to Anton. "Give it here!" he yelled and grabbed Anton's gun hand and began trying to wrestle it free.

"Should we help?" Rhonda asked from the doorway, watching the ruckus in the kitchen.

"We need to find Lara," Rita answered her sister. "Brad will handle Anton. Especially with Mark to help him." She grinned.

Rhonda looked down a long hallway striped in cozy shades of peppermint-pink and red and white that made her think of fireplaces singing with warmth during a gentle snow. "Lara could be anywhere. Maybe we should split up."

Rita watched Anton headbutt Mark in the nose as Brad continued to hold him down. Mark let out a loud whimper of pain but didn't let go of Anton's gun. "Your hero isn't so nerdy after all," she said and nodded her head down the hallway. "I'll take the second floor and you take the third floor. You heard Anton…there's hidden recording devices all over this mansion. I'm sure Lara has been listening to every word we've been saying."

Rhonda watched Mark get really mad and with a hard blow knocked the gun out of his hand. Anton let out a miserable cry of frustrated pain. As soon as he did, Brad pounced, yanked Anton's arms behind his back, and ordered Mark to grab a pair of handcuffs lying a few feet away. Mark scrambled to his feet, saw Rhonda smiling at him from the hallway, blushed, this is serious and time is of the essence. They are capturing criminals he wouldn't have stopped and waved at her and hurried to get the handcuffs. "Nice work," she called out to Mark.

"I...was just trying to help," Mark took the handcuffs over to Brad. He slapped them onto Anton, retrieved the man's gun, and stood up. "Good work," he said and patted Mark on his shoulder.

"We're going after Lara, Brad," Rhonda explained. "…and get Kathy out of the freezer."

"And take these handcuffs off me," Mae pleaded.

"That too," Rhonda added with an apologetic nod. She added, with a sparkle in her eyes, "You're my hero, Mark."

Mark smiled at Rhonda. Even with his adrenaline pumping and fear racing through his veins, Rhonda sure was pretty. Rita was pretty, too, and he knew the sisters were twins...but Rhonda's wit and easy jests made her the prettiest in his eyes. "I have to confess something to you... I crawled into the trunk of the sheriff's car," he explained. "My gut told me you were hiding a story. I'm sure glad I followed my gut."

"Maybe you can apologize over dinner sometime," Rhonda grinned and turned her attention to Rita. "Okay, sis, it's time to go catch us a rat."

Rita grinned at Rhonda. "Dinner?" she whispered.

Rhonda felt her cheeks blush deeply. "I...well..." she tried to speak and glanced at Mark. Brad grinned at the two of them.

"Oh, stop it," Rhonda complained and grabbed Rita's hand as they headed to the stairs.

"Okay," Rita said and the sisters hurried down the peppermint colored hallway.

They didn't know it, but they were headed toward a woman trapped in Rusty Lowly's room, unaware of what had transpired in the kitchen. Her attention was focused on an old man who was pointing a gun at her.

"You're one of the mean people who want to hurt me," Rusty told Lara in a scared voice. "Too much medicine... too much sleep...I swear I won't let you steal my memories...not anymore...never again!" All Lara could do was stare down the gun barrel pointed at her heart and wait to be shot by a crazy old man.

9

"Okay," Rhonda said, reaching the stairwell, "here is where we split up."

"Wish Lara hadn't taken our guns," Rita replied, looking uneasily over her shoulder. "If Lara spots us she is going to start shooting and we have no way to return fire."

Rhonda looked up. "We didn't play this smart, did we?" she asked in a miserable voice.

"I should have stayed hidden in the woods," Rita said, keeping her eyes peeled. "You could have acted as bait...I could have..." Rita stopped talking for a second. Then she looked at Rhonda. "My gut told me to leave the woods, Rhonda. My gut told me to come inside. Why? I don't know. But I've learned to listen and so have you." Rita focused back on the staircase. "We could have played this smarter, yes, but maybe we're exactly where we need to be."

"At least, let's hope so," Rhonda agreed. She drew in a steady breath. "Sometimes I get scared," she confessed, "really scared. But I'm not scared right now. As a matter of fact I have this...warm feeling inside. Like I'm being protected. The feeling came to me when we arrived back here from town. Can't really explain it, sis."

"Are you sure it's not about Mark Bricker showing up to be our hero?" Rita asked with a straight face, teasing yet serious.

Rhonda chuckled but shook her head no. "I feel like we're being helped," she insisted. "It's like...an angel is with us." Rhonda gazed around at the beautifully carved front door, the peppermint touches everywhere in the hallway around them, and then focused back on Rita. "I've felt this feeling before."

Rita felt a sweet peace touch her heart. "So have I," she said. "When we get ambushed, or right before we've been attacked, the same feeling I'm having now comes into my heart."

Rhonda nodded her head. "Yes," she said with a soft smile. "I guess we'll have to ask more questions about that later. We have a job to do, sis. Let's get to it. I'll take the third floor and you take the second floor. But be careful, because Lara was supposed to be checking in on the patients."

"But if she's been listening to us talk in the kitchen, it's more likely she's on the third floor hidden in an office, listening in," Rita pointed out.

"Fifty-fifty chance," Rhonda agreed. She looked Rita in the eyes with a love that communicated certain things that only twins could understand.

Looking at Rhonda and then making her way up the staircase. When she reached the second level, she looked at Rhonda, smiled, and veered off to her right, and entered a maze of hallways.

"Please be careful," Rhonda whispered, watching Rita vanish down the hallway. Once Rita was out of sight she climbed up to the third floor, looked to her right and then to her left, and decided to track down Mae's upper floor offices. "If I don't get lost first," she whispered. But as she walked down a short hallway that branched off into two longer hallways she felt like a strong hand was guiding her every step.

As Rhonda began working her way toward Mae's office, Rita entered a short hallway on the second floor with two doors. "Okay," she paused, "if I remember correctly, Mae said each hallway holds two rooms...Rusty's room must be farther back." Rita carefully stepped up to a door, feeling like a child caught inside the belly of a peppermint monster, and tried the doorknob. "Locked," she whispered and tried the second door. "Locked again." She felt badly for the poor residents locked inside but knew they were safer staying inside their rooms than evacuating, for the moment.

Using extreme caution, she moved on and found a second hallway, tried the two doors, found them locked as well, and finally made her way in the direction that led to

Rusty's room. As she entered the hallway Rita heard Rusty yell: "You're not going to steal my memories!"

Rita quickly pressed her back against the left wall and crept down to Rusty's door. The door was open just enough to allow Rita to see Lara standing with her hands held out in front of her, cornered in the room. "I'm not here to hurt you," she said in a voice that actually, to Rita's shock, held fear. Rita didn't think Lara was capable of fear. Lara pointed down at the floor. "My guns are on the floor, Mr. Lowly...you can see that, yes?"

Rusty kept his gun pointed at Lara. "You will not hurt me anymore!" he hollered in a hoarse voice. "I...I don't..." Rusty shook his head, fighting away the dark clouds trying to cover his mind. "I know who you are...what you want..."

Rita watched Rusty fight the medicine Noel had poisoned him with. The substance was strong enough to make the poor man forget why he was holding a gun. "Hang on, Rusty...fight it," Rita begged in a whisper. "Don't let the poison win."

Rusty looked at the gun he was holding in confused surprise. "You're...you want to hurt me...I know it...I know..." he tried to speak, his voice becoming weaker and weaker.

Lara watched Rusty's eyes grow dim and knew that the old man was slowly forgetting who she was. "Mr. Lowly, you need to lay down and rest," she said in a flat voice, all her fear gone now.

Rusty continued to stare at his gun. "Why...am I holding this?" he asked as the dark cloud finally covered his mind. He looked up at Lara with confusion, stumbling a little in his stupor. "Who are you?" he asked. "Are you one of the nurses?"

"No," Rita whispered in a miserable voice.

Lara lowered her hands. "I'm your friend, don't you recognize me?" she lied and took a step toward Rusty. "You need to give me your gun and lay down. You've had a very difficult day."

"I'm…I'm sorry…I don't know you…"But Rusty's hands grew so tired, he lowered his gun automatically as he shook his head. "You'd like my sister. My sister always hated the sight of guns. Said guns needed to be… hammered into plowshares…" He blinked and looked around him.

Lara took another step toward Rusty. She held out her right hand. "Give me your gun," she coaxed.

Rita knew she had to act. She closed her eyes, whispered a prayer, and then burst into Rusty's room with speed and power that even surprised her. Lara spun around in time to see Rita dive to the floor and snatch up one of the three guns lying on the floor. Rita rolled into a firing stance and immediately aimed for Lara.

Furious, Lara quickly grabbed Rusty, pulling the old man into her arms with no notice for his shock and pain. She shook her head at Rita. "No, no, no," she ordered in a deadly voice.

Rita watched Lara snatch Rusty's gun out of his hands. "Take it easy," Rita said.

Lara jammed Rusty's gun into his side. "What are you doing?" Rusty asked, gasping in pain. "I thought you were…a friend."

"Shut up," Lara hissed. "You," she ordered Rita, "put down the gun and stand up."

Rita glanced at the gun in her hand. The gun she was holding belonged to Rhonda. "I always shoot to the far right with her gun," Rita thought to herself with a sinking feeling in her heart.

"Put the gun down!" Lara yelled.

Rita kept her eyes on the gun and then, just as she was prepared to drop it, she saw Rusty's eyes suddenly clear as if the medicine that was poisoning his mind had been yanked out of his bloodstream. "Rusty?" she asked.

Rusty stared at Rita. "Do it," Rusty told Rita in a voice that sounded younger and stronger. He obviously didn't mean for her to drop the gun. His eyes danced with fire and fury that said, *You can't let this evil woman leave the room.*

"Rusty?" Rita repeated.

"Drop the gun!" Lara hollered at Rita.

Rita ignored Lara and continued to stare into Rusty's eyes. She saw the brilliant, brave police officer there who had been pushed down behind so many doses of poisonous medication. Somehow he had managed to push through.

"My uniforms…are not a costume," Rusty told Rita and lifted his right hand and pointed at his vintage police jacket and badges hanging on the wall with his old patrol cap. "My commitment…ran true blue. Duty first." He pointed to the bullet in the shadow box, the one that had nearly ended his life. His voice was quiet, still old and weakened, but his eyes and words were lucid and strong.

Rita glanced down. "Duty first," she whispered and then, to Lara's shock, bolted to her feet and aimed the gun right at Lara again. "Put down the gun and release Rusty...now!"

Lara took a step back toward the window, dragging Rusty with her. "I'll kill him!" she yelled at Rita.

"You may kill Mr. Lowly," Rita told Lara in a calm voice, "but that's the risk that a cop takes to take down scum like you. And I'll make sure you never leave this room alive. Now drop your gun." Rita nodded her head toward the room's door. "Anton is down in the kitchen with handcuffs on him. It's over, Lara."

"You're lying!"

"If I'm lying, how do you explain me being here?" Rita asked. "Surely Anton wouldn't have simply let me walk out of the kitchen alive, right?" Rita focused her attention on Lara's eyes. "Kathy Stein confessed the truth. She confessed that you were going to kill Anton in exchange for Lynn Hogan's money. Not a nice thing for a wife to do to her husband."

"You're lying!" Lara yelled again.

"Kathy Stein is going to testify in a court of law that she made a deal with you, Lara," Rita continued, pushing the tough woman into a state of panic. "She is going to testify that you were going to kill not only Anton but Mae, Noel, and Beth to cover your tracks and hers. And let me remind you, Kathy is married to a prominent lawyer who knows some pretty powerful people. By the time he's finished, she'll be free as a bird and you'll be at the bottom of a very dark and deep hole. But I think you know that, don't you? That's why you were going to kill Kathy once she forced Mae to give her the money. After all, what mother wouldn't protect her child...especially a child with Downs syndrome, vulnerable and all alone like Mae's daughter would be...you make me sick."

Lara's eyes grew wide with shock. "So it is true," she said, "Kathy betrayed me. That stupid idiot…"

"Kathy Stein is only interested in her own self-preservation, Lara," Rita explained and then decided to really shake Lara up. "Don't make this situation any worse. You're only guilty of killing Lynn Hogan—"

"I did not kill that woman," Lara snapped at Rita. "But...I saw it happen."

"Oh?" Rita asked, keeping her voice calm. "What did you see?"

"You will not believe me."

"Try me," Rita pressed Lara.

Lara narrowed her eyes, her chest heaving as she tried to think of a way out of her situation. She had almost relaxed her hold on Rusty by now. "Lynn Hogan was dying of cancer," she told Rita, dropping her voice into a lifeless whisper. "Early this morning she went down to the kitchen, took a knife, and went back to her room. I watched her on the hidden cameras I have installed." Lara locked eyes with Rita. "I see everything from my hidden space in the attic...every word, every call…"

"Get on with it," Rita ordered.

Lara sighed. "I watched Lynn go back into her room. Minutes later, this old man arrives at her door, maybe for a visit? When she didn't answer his knock, he went into her room….but by then it was too late. He found her dead on her bed. The woman had...killed herself."

Rita looked at Rusty. As she did, the man's eyes filled with grief and shock. She knew then that he had used his last ounce of strength to aid her, and his eyes might never clear again.

"I saw the knife," Rusty told Rita in a shaky voice. "I...didn't know what to do. Lynn told me in confidence that she wanted to end her life before the cancer did...I didn't believe her...and I never told anyone because every time I remembered, that kitchen woman came to my room and I would fall asleep...and..." The poison in Rusty reached into his mind and fogged over his memory. "I...I am so tired now…nurse, is it time for bed? I'm sorry, what was I saying?"

"You said enough," Rita whispered in a loving voice. "You're a real hero, Officer Lowly."

"You see? I didn't kill her," Lara snapped at Rita. "The old woman ended her own life."

Rita nodded her head. "Then don't make this situation any worse than it is, Lara. Let go of Rusty. Put down the gun and give yourself up peacefully."

Lara stared into Rita's eyes and saw that the cop wasn't going to let her leave the room...not without a fight. She also saw that the cop staring her down was prepared to fire at her at any second. As tough as Lara was on the outside, on the inside she feared for her life and wasn't prepared to shoot it out with a woman who had years of experience dealing with criminals. "No shoot-outs…I'm no Wyatt Earp," she said in an angry voice and slowly dropped her gun.

"Rusty, go lay down," Rita ordered kindly.

Lara let go of Rusty. Rusty looked at her with confused eyes, and then simply walked to his bed and laid down, drawing his crocheted comforter over himself with a happy sigh.

"I will go peacefully," Lara told Rita.

Rita motioned for the door, chagrined that she didn't have handcuffs to secure the dangerous woman. "Out in the hallway."

Lara nodded her head and walked toward it. As she did, and idea struck her panicked mind. In a sudden burst of fear and energy, she grabbed the doorknob and spun out into the hallway, managing to slam the door closed before Rita could reach it. Fearing that bullets would start flying through the door at any second, Lara turned and fled. As she did, an iron fireplace poker crashed down on her head. The last thing Lara remembered before crumpling down onto the floor was seeing Rita's face grinning down at her.

What she didn't know is that it wasn't Rita at all, but her twin sister Rhonda. "She swings and she hits a home run!" Rhonda yelled and began spinning and waving her arms in a silly victory dance.

Rita yanked Rusty's door open and stepped out. She spotted her sister doing a goofy dance and Lara lying unconscious on the floor. "Fifty-fifty," she grinned.

Rhonda held up the fireplace iron in her right hand. "Fifty-fifty, sis. I saw you on the monitors from the office upstairs…I had to improvise."

Rita laughed, "You're my hero."

Rhonda hugged Rita right back with fierce strength and relief. "Tomorrow you can buy me a funnel cake," she smiled.

"Tomorrow, we hide from Brad," Rita said with a grimace. "Could you hear us on the monitors? Rusty didn't kill Lynn. She ...committed suicide, Rhonda. The woman was dying of cancer."

Rhonda stopped smiling. "No, the nurse station monitors have no sound. Oh, how awful."

Rita nodded her head and then pointed down at Lara. "We need to tie her up, I don't have any handcuffs, do you?" As they searched for a tie or belt in Rusty's closet to improvise with, Rita felt the warm feeling in her heart slowly begin to fade away. "Uh...Rhonda..."

"I feel it, too," Rhonda whispered and simply closed her eyes. "Maybe Miss Katherine's spirit was the angel watching over us, Rita." She looked at her sister with love and affection. "Rita, I love Clovedale Falls, and I'm so grateful this is our new home."

Rita felt a smile touch her lips. "Me, too," she said in a whisper before her tears of happiness got the best of her. "I think this life is absolutely perfect for us. Even if it has its twists and turns sometimes."

"I feel the exact same way," Rhonda whispered.

Down the hall, Nurse Mae whispered, "Me, too," without being seen. Then she smiled and hurried back down to the kitchen with silent steps, feeling Miss Katherine's warm spirit of love everywhere around her.

10

Billy threw an apple at a red and white bullseye, missed, and began mumbling under his breath. "Ain't no lousy bullseye going to get the best of Billy Northfield," he said and pointed at the chubby man perched on a wooden plank over a tank of frigid cold water. "Mayor, you're going for a swim if it's the last thing I do!"

Rita let out a giggle, took a bite of delicious funnel cake, and watched Billy throw another apple at the metal bullseye as a gentle wind rippled the hem of her soft blue dress. "That's your tenth apple, Billy."

The next apple Billy shot at the bullseye missed. Billy kicked the ground with his work boot and then looked down at a wooden basket full of apples. "I paid for these here apples and my daddy always said you get what you pay for. I ain't leaving until that mayor goes for a swim."

"May I have a try?" Rita asked, the autumn wind begin playing in her hair. The wind felt sweet and peaceful, carrying the smells of funnel cakes, apple cider, pumpkin pies, and leaves to her nose.

"I reckon so," Billy said, "but don't go getting disappointed if you miss." He turned to hand her an apple and hesitated, then hesitantly reached out and brushed an dab of funnel cake sugar off the tip of her adorable nose.

Rita handed Billy her funnel cake with a smile and took the apple from him. She looked around at a fairground full of happy visitors and smiled. Sure, the world was changing and the tourists came more than ever through the tiny town, but so what? Clovedale Falls would never change deep down. When all the tourists were gone, Clovedale Falls would simply yawn and go back to bed, cradling its people with loving, warm arms. "I won't be disappointed," Rita promised and took aim carefully at the metal target.

Billy stood back and bit down on his lip. "Now...just aim at the bullseye," he told Rita in a worried voice, "eye on the apple...don't worry about hitting it your first try...just kinda get a feel for the apple."

"Got it," Rita smiled. Then she wound back her arm and let the apple fly free. The apple zoomed through the air, struck the bullseye with a loud clang, and dropped to the ground. A loud buzzer exploded into the air and the wooden plank dropped out from under the mayor, dropping the poor man down into the tank of cold water. Everyone watching burst out into excited applause and laughter.

LET'S BAKE A DEAL

"I hit it, Billy! I hit the bullseye!"

"Well, I'll be a monkey's uncle," Billy said in an amazed voice. "So you did."

Rita smiled, took her funnel cake from him, and laughed. "I couldn't have done it without your help, Billy. Your turn."

"What did I do?"

"I had to watch you throw eleven apples first, didn't I? Maybe that taught me something," Rita said and reached over to brush a piece of grass off his shoulder.

Billy looked into Rita's beautiful eyes and smiled. Rita sure was a pretty woman, he thought—but it was her heart that was prettier than anything he had ever seen. "I reckon I better stop while the stopping's good," he said and scratched the back of his neck. "My daddy always told me to let the ladies win. Reckon I'd be better off making an apple pie of them apples instead of letting my pride waste them."

"Okay," Rita giggled and looked around. She spotted Rhonda standing at a game booth with Mark. Mark was trying to toss beans into small fishbowls full of brightly colored water. Rhonda, she could tell, was teasing his ear off. "Poor Mark."

Billy spotted them teasing Mark. Mark, the poor soul, was desperately trying to impress a pretty woman wearing a pink dress that made her beauty gleam like the sunset on a pretty summer evening. "Your sister ain't making it easy on that fella," Billy joked. "I've known Mark for a good many years and I ain't never seen him work so hard to impress a gal...a woman before."

Rita nudged Billy with her elbow. "You can call us gals," she teased.

"Oh," Billy blushed and took off his hat, rubbed his forehead, and blushed even more. "Guess it's the old Georgia boy in me. I don't mean no offense."

"None taken," Rita quickly replied and nodded toward Rhonda. "We gals understand a compliment when we get one."

Billy put his hat back on, watched a group of kids run up to the dunk tank. "Hey, look at all these apples someone paid for and left here!" one of the kids yelled and grabbed an apple out of the wooden basket Billy had left behind. "Let's make that man go for a swim." The poor mayor sputtered as he shivered a little on his seat and wiped the water from his eyes and crooked his fingers at the kids as if to say, come and get me.

Rita looked at Billy, who merely grinned. "Oh, let those rascals have them apples. Be good for the mayor to take more than one bath today. It'll teach him a good lesson for not fixing that pothole on the road leading out to my farm."

Rita watched the kids begin throwing apples at the bullseye. The poor mayor flinched and waited to go for another swim. "Maybe we should go help Mark win a

LET'S BAKE A DEAL

prize for Rhonda," she said. Billy agreed and walked Rita over to the booth where Rhonda stood. "How's he doing?"

Rhonda took a drink of her hot spiced apple cider and nodded at Mark. "Ten dollars and not a single bean," she teased. "Mark, don't get frustrated on my account."

Mark, frustrated that he couldn't land a single bean in a silly fish bowl, claimed that the wind was interfering. Billy patted Mark on his shoulder. "My daddy always said don't blame your boots just because you can't dance."

Mark chuckled, looked down at the beans he was holding. "I guess so, Billy," he said and tossed the whole handful of beans at the fishbowls without aiming. "I give up already!" One of the beans landed in a fishbowl. "Just my luck," Mark laughed again.

An older man wearing a brown button-up shirt and old fishing hat smiled at Mark. He grabbed a prize apple pie, handed it to Mark, and winked. "For your girl."

"Oh...she's not my girl," Mark stammered. "We're just...here together." He gulped and handed the pie to Rhonda, whose smile lit a small fire inside Mark.

The old man pointed at the gray suit Mark was wearing. "Known you since you were Bricker's boy, kid. I've never seen you dressed so fancy before," he said and tossed Mark another wink.

Rhonda smiled at Rita. Rita smiled back. But her smile quickly faded when she saw Sheriff Brad walking toward them with a serious look on his face. "Oh no, it's Brad," she groaned.

Rhonda spun around, spotted Brad, and tried to think of a quick escape route. But Brad was too close and captured her before any escape could take place. "I'm glad I found you ladies," Brad said. "I have some news for you."

"No more murder cases," Rhonda begged. "Brad, can't you see my sister and I are on a double date?"

"A date?" Mark asked.

"A date?" Billy mirrored Mark's confusion. "Why I thought we were just...walking around together?" Billy looked at Rita. Rita blushed. Billy nearly fainted. Mark looked quite pale but ecstatic.

"No murder," Brad told Rhonda in an easy voice. "Everything is quiet up at the retirement home, now that the place belongs to Mae." Billy looked at the old man. "Hank, how are you?"

"Old and loving life," Hank joked and handed Brad a homemade miniature apple pie. "Wife will be upset if I come home with her pies. Take an extra, will you, Sheriff?"

Brad took the pie. "You bet," he said.

"So what has you wandering around besides enjoying the festival?" Rita asked.

"I have news about Rusty," Brad explained. He took the plastic wrap off his tiny apple pie, took a bite, and smiled. "Good, Hank. My compliments to the wife."

"What about Rusty?" Rita asked.

"The hospital in Atlanta called Mae," Brad explained and motioned for Rhonda and Rita to start walking with him. "The doctors have managed to stabilize Rusty's condition now that he's off that medication he was poisoned with." Brad took another bite of his apple pie as the autumn winds blew a gust of leaves past. The winds were turning colder, but winter held at bay. "Rusty is old," he continued, "and even without such an ordeal he was having memory problems. That's something the doctors can't fix. But Mae has told me that Rusty is being given a new medicine that is going to help his memory."

"That's great news," Rita said and glanced over her shoulder. Billy and Mark were slowly following behind looking like the two sweetest, clumsiest, lovestruck men she had ever seen.

"I guess that's good news," Rhonda sighed. "It's very sad that the new medicine can only do so much. I suppose memory loss is normal at his age, though."

"Indeed," Brad told Rhonda as they walked past lines of families waiting at a funnel cake stand. "We can't stop age."

"Tell me about it," Rhonda said feeling her feet aching, wishing she had worn her running shoes instead of pink kitten heels to match her dress. The things a woman does to impress her nerdy but sweet date.

Rita looked at Brad. "Brad, what about Kathy Stein?" she asked. "Any news?"

Brad frowned. "Kathy Stein's husband is using every trick up his sleeve, calling every person in power he knows in order to save his wife. At best, the woman will get a slap on the wrist, maybe a few hours of community service, and that's it."

"That's what we assumed," Rita replied.

Brad shrugged his shoulders. "At least she was forced to surrender the retirement home as a condition of settling her initial charges."

"She did that out of guilt," Rhonda pointed out. "Kathy could have fought Mae about that in court but decided to make it look like an act of charity instead. Guilt does strange things to a person. Seems like Kathy Stein, as horrible as she was, does have a little conscience left. Even if she was doing it for the publicity, maybe, instead of the right reasons."

"I'm glad no matter why she did it," Rita pointed out. "Mae deserves to own the mansion. She's a part of that place. Miss Katherine would have wanted it that way."

"I agree," Brad said and finished off his apple pie. "Mae is considering bringing her daughter to Clovedale Falls to live with her. She ain't sure yet. We'll just have to wait and see." Brad stopped walking and stretched in the bright sunshine. "Anton and Lara Peterson are being extradited to Russia before they serve time here. Seems those two have a pile of crimes that they'll have to answer to before the American justice system can get ahold of them."

"Really?" Rita asked in a relieved voice. "Brad, that's great news."

"It sure is," Rhonda smiled. "Two less people to worry about."

Brad looked at Billy and Mark to make sure they weren't listening. Billy was looking around like he was more interested in the activities going on. Mark tried to pretend he wasn't taking mental notes for a news article.

"Beth and Noel are in hot water," Brad explained. "Those two are going to get hefty prison sentences. Shame that the woman who hired them will only get a slap on the wrist."

"It's her connections," Rita said in a disgusted voice. "Kathy Stein may have a touch of conscience left but she deserves prison for her crimes against Rusty. We all know she orchestrated that whole plan, even if she didn't do the dirty work."

Brad nodded his head. "Yep," he said and watched a group of kids race to line up for one of the carnival rides. "I reckon justice will come to her in one way or another. We all reap what we sow in this life."

"I guess so," Rita agreed. She stood still, allowed the wind to caress her face, and then looked at Billy. Poor Billy was still staring up at the sky. "Is…that all you came to tell us, Brad?"

"Yeah," Brad said, "but there is one more thing."

"Uh oh," Rhonda fretted.

"It's nothing bad," Brad assured Rhonda. "You both know that the coroner ruled Lynn Hogan's death a suicide."

"Yes," Rita said.

"And you both know that Mae has inherited the woman's wealth?"

"Of course," Rhonda told Brad.

Brad nodded his head. "Well, Mae wants you ladies to come up the retirement home next week for a little get-together. She said she has a reward for you ladies."

"Reward?" Rita asked. "But we can't accept—"

"Now, now." Brad shook his head. "Don't go looking a gift horse in the mouth. Mae said something about how trusting someone can really pay off."

Rita and Rhonda looked at each other. "Pay off?"

Brad smiled. "Yep," he said and looked around. "Well, I better get back on duty. I'll see you ladies later."

They watched Brad walk away. "Everything okay?" Billy called out.

Rita turned around, spotted Billy standing like a kid waiting for a treat, and smiled. "Yes, everything is okay, Billy."

Rhonda walked back to Mark and smiled. "What should we do now?"

Billy pointed up at the clouds beginning to crowd the sky. "Chester told me rain was moving in," he said. "I reckon it'll be raining in about another hour."

"Then we better hurry up and check out the craft booths," Rita told Rhonda in an urgent voice. "Billy," she said, "you and Mark better come along. We're going to need you to carry what we buy."

"Oh yes," Rhonda giggled, "us gals need two strong men to carry our stuff for us." Rhonda winked at Rita. Rita winked back.

Billy looked at Mark. "My daddy always said that when mama started to buy stuff, better go fetch yourself a wheelbarrow."

Mark looked at Rhonda with stars in his eyes. For whatever reason, this lovely woman had agreed to spend the day with him. The idea that she had referred to it as a date not too long ago felt like a warm blanket for his heart. "I don't mind, Billy," he confessed and smiled at Rhonda. "A pretty girl is worth all the trouble in the world."

Rhonda blushed at Mark's compliment. Rita grinned at Billy. Billy grinned back and nodded his head. "Well, we better get to shopping. Besides, Chester is sitting in the truck and he gets mighty upset when it rains."

"He sure does," Rita giggled and looped her arm through Billy's. "Maybe after we get through shopping, you sweet men can take us to the diner for a bite to eat?"

Billy smiled from ear to ear. "Now that's a mighty fine idea. My belly is hungering for some real food. What do you say, Mark?"

Mark looked into Rhonda's sparkling eyes. "You bet," he smiled.

Rhonda blushed again and then slapped Mark on his arm playfully. "Come on, silly," she said, full of joy.

Rita watched her sister pull Mark forward into the crowd and smiled. "You know, Billy," she said and slowly began walking, "I'm sorry we had to step away to talk to the sheriff a bit ago. I guess life can have its ugly detours at times."

"It sure can," Billy agreed.

Rita spotted a toddler boy walking along with a balloon, holding his mother's hand. "But life sure can be beautiful, too, even if the world is changing all the time...there's still beauty all around us."

Billy spotted a little girl holding her father's hand and skipping across the grassy fairgrounds. He smiled. "I reckon we if look past all the muddy parts we might find a little rose growing," he said.

Rita looked up into Billy's warm eyes and a tender weight touched her heart. "You're one of those roses yourself, Billy Northfield." She walked through the fairgrounds holding onto the arm of a good man, finally at peace.

What Rita and Rhonda didn't know as they basked in the autumn day was that something far darker than a rainstorm was brewing out at Billy's farm and poor Billy was going to be the number one suspect for murder. So for now the leaves danced in the air and the smell of the Pumpkin Festival sang in people's hearts.

ABOUT WENDY

Wendy Meadows is a USA Today bestselling author whose stories showcase witty women sleuths. To date, she has published dozens of books, which include her popular Sweetfern Harbor series, Sweet Peach Bakery series, and Alaska Cozy series, to name a few. She lives in the "Granite State" with her husband, two sons, two mini pig and a lovable Labradoodle.

If you enjoyed this book, please take a few minutes to leave a review. Authors truly appreciate this, and it helps other readers decide if the book might be for them. Thank you!

Get in touch with Wendy
www.wendymeadows.com

CPSIA information can be obtained
at www.ICGtesting.com
Printed in the USA
BVHW090757111220
595376BV00010B/620